Five Nights at Freddy's™

FAZBEAR FRIGHTS #9

THE PUPPET CARVER

Five Nights at Freddy's™

FAZBEAR FRIGHTS #9
THE PUPPET CARVER

BY

SCOTT CAWTHON
ELLEY COOPER

Scholastic Inc.

Copyright © 2021 by Scott Cawthon. All rights reserved.

Photo of TV static: © Klikk/Dreamstime

All rights reserved. Published by Scholastic Inc., *Publishers since 1920.* SCHOLASTIC and associated logos are trademarks and/or registered trademarks of Scholastic Inc.

The publisher does not have any control over and does not assume any responsibility for author or third-party websites or their content.

No part of this publication may be reproduced, stored in a retrieval system, or transmitted in any form or by any means, electronic, mechanical, photocopying, recording, or otherwise, without written permission of the publisher. For information regarding permission, write to Scholastic Inc., Attention: Permissions Department, 557 Broadway, New York, NY 10012.

This book is a work of fiction. Names, characters, places, and incidents are either the product of the author's imagination or are used fictitiously, and any resemblance to actual persons, living or dead, business establishments, events, or locales is entirely coincidental.

Library of Congress Cataloging-in-Publication Data available

978-1-338-73999-2 (Trade ISBN)
978-1-338-78488-6 (Variant Cover ISBN)
1 2021

Printed in the U.S.A.

First printing 2021 • Book design by Jeff Shake

23

TABLE OF CONTENTS

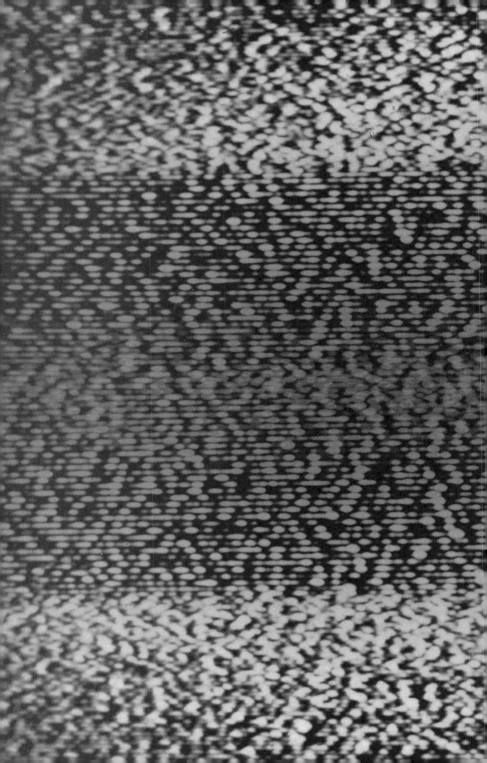

THE PUPPET CARVER

Onstage, the banjo-strumming animatronic pig slowed in its movements, emitted a sputtering sound, and then ground to a halt.

"Really? Another one?" Jack yelled. The stupid pig was the third animatronic to break in less than a month. And fixing those things cost money. Money that Jack didn't have.

This place was bleeding him dry. When he bought it three years ago, he had thought that the Pizza Playground, a kiddie pizzeria complete with games and animatronics, would be a great investment. Pizza, games, talking and singing animal characters— those were all things kids loved, right? And parents were always looking for ways to keep their little brats entertained, especially on their birthdays. He had anticipated a lot of birthday business.

But the fact was, the kids weren't showing up, and Jack didn't know why. Was it because parents these days packed their kids' schedules so full of sports and lessons that there was no time left for mindless entertainment? Or did kids today just prefer mindless entertainment of a different sort on their computers or video game consoles? Whatever the reason, Jack was losing money like it was water pouring through a sieve. Just this morning, he had to order the kitchen staff to throw away expired ingredients for the pizzas nobody was going to eat. And now he had to figure out how to pay for repairs of the animatronics that nobody was going to see.

"Porter! Sage! Get out here!" Jack yelled. He was so angry and stressed he felt his face heating up. He remembered the doctor telling him to be mindful of his blood pressure, but how could you keep your blood pressure down when everything around you was flying out of control?

Porter came out from behind the stage, and Sage

emerged from the custodial closet. Both were in their early twenties, young enough to be Jack's sons. But these boys were no sons of his. *What a couple of losers*, Jack thought as they shambled up to him like dogs making a futile attempt to please their master. Well, Jack wasn't *pleased* with either one of them. Porter, the short one with glasses, was a handyman who was supposed to be in charge of the animatronics. He claimed to be some kind of inventor, and when he was not ineptly trying to follow Jack's orders, he was always tinkering with the tools and equipment in the storage room. Sage, the tall one who wore his long black hair in braids, was supposed to keep the place clean. He fancied himself a writer. He spent his breaks sitting at a table in the dining area, hunched over a notebook, scribbling away on his so-called "novel."

Clearly neither of these idiots are going anywhere, Jack thought. They were lucky he saw fit to pay them minimum wage and let them take home leftover pizza.

"The pig's busted," Jack said. "Take it back to storage."

"Wow, those things are dropping like flies," Sage said, looking up at the almost-empty stage.

"I don't need your commentary, Captain Obvious," Jack said. "I just need your muscles to take the porker to the storage room."

"Yes, sir," Sage said, but he looked like he was suppressing the urge to roll his eyes.

Jack couldn't stand insubordination.

"Well, soon all your animatronic problems will be solved anyway," Porter said, stepping up onto the stage to help move the broken figure. "I'm almost finished with the prototype of my machine. It will create low-cost but highly functional animatronics made from only an inexpensive slab of wood. You're going to be amazed, Jack!"

"I'll believe it when I see it," Jack muttered. Something about the little guy's ungrounded optimism was especially irritating.

Porter grinned like he was being issued a particularly satisfying challenge. "Oh, you'll see it. And you'll believe it." He turned to Sage. "You ready to lift this thing? Let's do it on the count of three. One . . . two . . ."

With Sage's help, Porter set down the deceased pig animatronic in a corner of the storage room. "I get so tired of the way that ogre talks to us," Porter said. "Once I get a patent on my invention and find a buyer, I'm going to be out of here so fast I'll leave a dust trail."

"And I'll be stuck here eating your dust," Sage said with a sigh. "Maybe someday you'll take pity on me and invite me to your mansion and feed me a meal.

You know, remember your old coworker who's still living on leathery reheated pizza slices."

Porter gave Sage a pat on the shoulder. "Hey, you won't need my pity. You'll get your novel published. Your book will be on the bestseller list. You'll tour the country doing signings. No more reheated pizza for you."

Sage grinned shyly. "You really think it's good enough to be published?"

"Of course I do!" Porter said. He was happy to give his buddy a pep talk, but it was an honest pep talk. Sage really was talented. "It's way better than a lot of published books I've read. And it's not just me who thinks so. Your creative writing teacher says so, too, right?" Porter and Sage attended the local community college together, though they majored in radically different fields—mechanical engineering for Porter and English for Sage.

Sage nodded. "She's been very complimentary of it, yeah."

"Well, there you go! And actually, I've got to say, I find your work not just entertaining but inspiring. My invention is partially inspired by your novel."

Sage raised an eyebrow. "How's that?"

"Well, *The Puppet Carver* is about a wooden man who wants to be real, right?"

Sage nodded.

"Well, my Puppet Carver takes an ordinary piece

of wood and transforms it into something that seems alive." He hadn't heard Jack yelling, so he figured the grumpy boss must be temporarily distracted. Porter pulled back the glittery purple curtain that hid his invention along with several broken animatronics. "Come check it out. If Jack comes back here, I'll pretend to be working on the animatronics, and you can pretend to be cleaning something."

Sage smiled. "You're a bad influence, Porter." He followed the shorter man behind the old curtain that had probably hung in front of the stage once.

"Here it is!" Porter said, gesturing with a flourish to a clunky-looking piece of equipment. "The Puppet Carver!"

"It looks kind of like a giant wood chipper," Sage said.

"Well, that's the basic concept," Porter said in a salesman voice. "But it does so much more!" Like a wood chipper, the puppet carver had an opening where the wood was fed in. But what happened once the wood was inside the machine was far more sophisticated. Once he got a few of the kinks worked out, Porter planned to apply for a patent. He hoped that the Puppet Carver would be the first of many patented inventions. "Here, help me load this log into it, and I'll show you what happens."

"Okay," Sage said, but he sounded a little unsure. "This is a safe piece of equipment, right?"

"The safest!" Porter said. "All the sharp parts are on the inside."

The machine was a tall, vertical metal cylinder with a sliding door that was opened by pushing a button. When Porter pushed the button, the door slid open, revealing a human-size compartment that was surrounded by metal blades. Together, Sage and Porter hefted a five-foot cedar log and stood it on its end inside the compartment.

Porter pushed a button. "And now we wait."

The machine hummed to life, then grew louder and louder. It whirred, then sputtered, then roared.

"Is it supposed to be making all those sounds?" Sage yelled over the noise.

The mechanical noises were like music to Porter. He smiled. "It's working perfectly."

After less than a minute of noisy shaking, the machine grew quiet.

"Behold!" Porter pointed to the inner compartment. "Here's the best part."

"I'm beholding," Sage said, sounding like he wasn't sure what to think yet.

Porter pushed the button and the door slid open, revealing a fully jointed, wooden, humanlike figure. "Now I just have to give a gentle tug." Porter grabbed the wooden figure by its shoulders and pulled, then pulled harder.

Sage laughed. "It looks like you're helping the machine give birth."

"That's exactly what I'm doing," Porter said. He gave a mighty pull, and the figure inside the machine finally turned loose. Porter pulled it the rest of the way out and then set it up on its feet.

Porter knew that some people would describe the figure as crude, but to him it was beautiful. It was in the shape of a small man. The simple wooden figure reminded him of the drawing models they had used in his high school art class. Even though it was basic, it could still be extremely useful to someone like Grumpy Boss. Put the figure in a fuzzy suit to resemble a bunny or a fox or a bear, and you'd have a low-cost animatronic that would be perfect for the pizzeria.

"Okay, okay," Sage said, smiling. "I have to admit that's pretty cool."

"Oh, you haven't even seen the cool part yet," Porter said. "Just wait."

He pushed a button on the wooden figure's lower back, and it slowly started to move. It turned its head to the left, then to the right. It lifted its arms so it looked like it was reaching out for a hug.

"Whoa," Sage said, sounding amazed. "You made this all by yourself?"

Porter laughed. "Yup, all by myself like a big boy.

It's incredibly cost efficient. If you can afford a log, you can make an animatronic."

"You know, I think Jack might actually be impressed by this," Sage said, walking in a circle around the animatronic and watching its movements.

"I hope so," Porter said, knowing that the boss wasn't easy to impress. "It would be nice to get some respect around here. And maybe a little money, too."

"No doubt," Sage said. "But if you keep it up with the inventions, you won't be hanging around this dump for long anyway. You're on your way, man."

"So are you," Porter said. Sage had let him read the first few chapters of his novel, and Porter had been blown away by his friend's vivid language and imagination.

"I hope so," Sage said. "I sure don't want to spend my best years in this place."

"Oh!" Porter said, looking back at the Puppet Carver. "I almost forgot an important step in the demonstration." He squatted down beside the machine. "After the puppet comes out, you want to slide out the drawer at the bottom here. It's full of all the sawdust and splinters left over from the carving process. If you don't empty it out, the machine won't work right the next time you use it." He dumped the contents of the compartment into the trash can.

"Kind of like the lint filter on the dryer?" Sage said.

"Exactly."

"Are there any people working in this place?" Jack's booming voice yelled from the dining area. "I've got tables that need wiping down and a stage that needs setting up!"

Sage chucked Porter on the shoulder. "I guess we're not quite ready for fame and fortune yet, huh?"

Porter laughed. "Nope. Not when there are tables to be wiped and animatronics to be arranged."

They headed for the dining area, prepared for a barrage of verbal abuse from Jack.

It was a good thing they were prepared.

"So does anybody besides me *work* here?" Jack yelled. His face was purple with rage.

If Porter liked Jack more, he'd worry about his health. The guy's blood pressure must be through the roof. "Sorry, sir. We were taking care of some stuff in the back."

"Well, people don't see the back! They see the front! And the front is a mess. The tables are dirty. You need to fix things up on the stage so it doesn't look like there are animatronics missing."

"That was actually what we were working on, sir—the animatronics," Porter said. "Soon all your problems with animatronics will be solved for a fraction of what you've been spending." Porter internally cringed to hear himself sounding like a TV infomercial, but his past experiences with Jack had taught him that the man liked cheesy marketing speech; he thought it "sounded smart."

"I won't hold my breath," Jack harrumphed.

"Well, you won't have to. How about I let you see it on Friday morning before we open?" Porter said. "I think I should have all the bugs worked out by then."

"You'd better," Jack said, which Porter decided to take for Jack's version of a *yes*. "So what are you standing around for? Get to work."

"Yes, sir." Sage grabbed a bucket of bleach water and a rag and started wiping down the tables. Porter climbed up on the stage and started fiddling with the animatronics.

Jack got up from his table. "I've got to take care of some things in the office, but I'll be back to check up on you."

"Yes, sir," Porter said, dragging an animatronic center stage.

Once Jack was safely out of earshot, Porter muttered, "Somebody must've spit in his oatmeal this morning."

"This morning and every morning," Sage said. "Have you ever seen the man in a good mood?"

Porter rolled his eyes. "Not once. I wonder if he ever is. Maybe when he's not a work? Do you think there's anything he does for fun?"

"Sure," Sage said, looking up from the table he

was wiping. "He kicks puppies, robs grandmothers, makes orphans cry."

Porter laughed. "We'd better be quiet or we'll get in trouble."

Sage grinned. "When *aren't* we in trouble?"

They worked quietly for a while. Once Porter had things working on the stage, he felt a strange presence in the room. The hair on the back of his neck prickled. He felt like he was being watched.

He turned around and saw he had been right. A little girl around four years old was standing right at the edge of the stage. She looked up at Porter with big brown eyes. "Hi," she said.

"Hi," Porter said. A few feet behind her were a man and a woman, presumably the little girl's parents. "Hi, folks," he added awkwardly. Customers had become such a rarity that it was always a surprise when they showed up.

The little girl pointed at the animatronic bear. "Is that Baron von Bear?"

"Yep, that's the baron," Porter said. Really, he should've had the curtain closed so that any kids who might show up wouldn't have seen the characters in their dormant state.

"Is he gonna sing?" the little girl asked.

"Yes," Porter said. "The first show's in fifteen minutes."

"Is there pizza?"

"Of course there's pizza." Porter swiped a few menus from the host's station and handed them to the family. "Why don't you folks sit at any table you want, and I'll go find you a server?"

Angie, the only server left in the place, was sitting in the kitchen doing her homework. She was studying to be a licensed practical nurse, she had told Porter, because this restaurant gig was obviously a dead end. Edwin, the cook, was playing on his phone.

"Hey, Ang," Porter said. "You've got a table of customers."

Angie looked up from her textbook. "Really? You mean I might actually earn *a tip* tonight?"

Porter grinned. "It's looking like it. Don't spend it all in one place."

"Hey, and I might actually get to cook something," Edwin said, pocketing his phone. "We need to use some of these ingredients. Half of them are about to go bad anyway."

Angie was on her feet. "I won't share that information with my one table of customers."

Edwin laughed. "Good idea."

A few more families trickled in over the course of the evening, but business was still slow, and Porter spent most of the night trying to look busy so Jack wouldn't yell at him too much. The mood in the place was all wrong. A children's pizza emporium was supposed to be loud and lively and full of laughter. But the only thing you were likely to hear in this place were Jack's outbursts.

It was always such a relief to walk out in the fresh night air after closing time. Porter, Sage, Angie, and Edwin left Jack and his anger inside, and instantly the mood was lighter.

"Say, do you guys want to get something to eat?" Porter asked. He probably should save what little money he had, but he couldn't face the thought of bolting down another pot of instant ramen noodles in his apartment.

There were murmurings of agreement.

"What do you want?" Porter asked.

"Not pizza!" everybody yelled in chorus.

It was a running joke. They ate so many leftover slices that they were all sick of them, but they kept on eating them because they were free. Actually paying to eat pizza—even good pizza—had become unimaginable.

They ended up at the Golden Heifer even though none of them had enough money for burgers and had to settle for grilled cheese or BLTs instead. They shared an order of fries between the four of them, which the tired-looking waitress placed in the middle of the table.

"Hey, you guys aren't looking for a cook, are you?" Edwin asked the waitress as she set down the ketchup bottle.

"Not right now, hon," she said. "But if you want to fill out an application, we'll put it on file."

"Thanks. I'll do that." Edwin flashed her a charming smile. After the waitress left, Edwin's smile faded. "I tell you what, guys. I'm pounding the pavement to find another job. If y'all want to keep on eating, you should start looking, too."

"You think Jack's going to fire us?" Angie asked, pouring out a puddle of ketchup on the fry plate.

"Well, that's a possibility, too," Edwin said, sipping his coffee. "But I think the place is gonna close down before Jack has a chance to fire us. I've worked in the restaurant business a lot longer than you kids have. I can tell when a place isn't long for this world. It gets the stink of death on it."

"Are you sure that's not just the stink of pepperoni past its expiration date?" Sage asked.

"Same difference," Edwin said, grabbing a french fry and dragging it through the shared puddle of ketchup. "If we were selling that pepperoni, it wouldn't be going bad, and we wouldn't be in danger of being out of a job."

"Wow, now I'm depressed," Angie said, stirring her soda with her straw.

"No need to get depressed," Edwin said. "You're in nursing school. You've got a good career ahead of you, and Porter and Sage are college boys. I'm the only one at this table who's looking down a dead-end street."

"Well, maybe you're not," Porter said. "I've just about finished my invention, which will bring the cost of animatronics way, way down. I'm showing it to Jack on Friday. If he doesn't have to keep replacing expensive animatronics, then he can pour his money into advertising and better food quality, maybe even buy a few new games. Then customers will start coming again."

"Well, I admire your optimism," Angie said, popping a french fry into her mouth. "I hope it pays off."

"I think it actually might," Sage said. "Porter showed it to me tonight. He's calling it the Puppet Carver because of my novel. It's pretty amazing." He grinned. "The invention, I mean, not my novel. Though the novel's pretty amazing, too."

"Your confidence is inspiring," Edwin said. He raised his soda glass. "Let's toast to a brighter future!"

"To a brighter future," the friends said, clinking glasses.

Porter and Sage shared a two-bedroom basement apartment. From the window, they could see the spectacular view of people's feet walking on the sidewalk above. The apartment was dark and damp with cheap paneling on the walls and ancient moss-colored carpet on the squeaky floor. The one thing you could say for it was that the rent was fairly cheap, especially with the two of them sharing it.

Tonight was the same as every other night. They got home. Sage went to his room to work on his novel. Porter went to his room to work on designs for his inventions. Porter drew and measured and made notes, working until he was so tired he could no longer hold his eyes open. Then he would collapse into bed, setting the alarm so he would wake up in time to get ready for the morning classes he took before returning to Abusive Pizza Land, as he called it, in the afternoon. It was a grueling schedule that wore him to the bone, but he kept on pushing, sure that he was on his way to something better. Meanwhile, Sage returned to his manuscript, typing in the dim glow of his desk lamp until late in the night.

from **The Puppet Carver**
a novel by Sage Brantley

Sylvester Pine emerged from the chamber as a perfect specimen. The first thing he saw were his hands, which were fully jointed. He watched himself curl them into fists, then straighten them back out and spread the fingers apart.

"Remarkable, yes?" his creator said.

Sylvester nodded.

"Would you like to see more of yourself?" his creator asked.

Sylvester nodded again.

His creator smiled. "You are programmed with the power of language, both the ability to comprehend and the ability to speak. When I ask you a question, please answer it with a yes or a no. Now . . . would you like to see more of yourself?"

"Yes," Sylvester said. The word slipped from his lips effortlessly.

"Good," his creator said. "Follow me."

Sylvester let his creator lead him to a large piece of glass he somehow knew was called a mirror. Sylvester regarded himself. He was a complete person, with symmetrical facial features and eyes that opened and closed. When he wished to move an arm or a leg, it moved according to his unspoken commands. He was not yet clothed, but when he was, he knew that he would strongly resemble a man with one exception. The surface of his face and body, unlike his creator's, was not soft and pliable because instead of flesh, he was made of smooth, solid wood.

"You're a handsome fellow," his creator said. "And a highly functional one. You can think. You can move. You can talk. You have three of the five senses regular humans have: sight, hearing, and smell."

"What senses am I missing?"

His creator shrugged. "Nothing very important. You don't have a sense of taste because you have no need to eat. And you don't have a sense of touch because we haven't been able to perfect the technology yet. But this isn't a wholly bad thing. You'll have no ability to feel heat or cold, *no ability to feel pain. In some ways, this lack makes you superior to those who have it."*

Sylvester touched his left hand with his right hand. Then he reached out and touched his creator on the shoulder.

His creator was right. Sylvester felt nothing.

Before Jack entered the house, he took off his shoes. Becky forbade wearing shoes inside because they might scuff the beautiful new hardwood floors. Jack understood this—he knew how much the new flooring had cost; he had paid for it—but taking off his shoes and holding them in his hands still made him feel strangely sneaky, as though he were a thief trying to break into his own house.

He walked into the newly remodeled home. The hardwood floors gleamed. The new living room furniture was sleek and modern (if not as comfortable as he would like). Becky loved to watch all those shows about redoing houses, and she had really put her heart and soul into making their comfy, older house look elegant and new.

But when Jack looked at his plush surroundings, all he could see was money flying out of his pockets.

He found Becky at the kitchen table, reading a home-and-garden magazine and sipping a diet soda. Even though it was late, she was still dressed in a designer blouse and dress slacks, her hair and makeup perfectly in order. Ever since she got the house looking the way she wanted it, it was like she had to look a certain way, too. No more lounging around in sweatpants. She had to match the decor.

She looked up from her magazine. "You know, I've been thinking we might want to knock down the wall between the living room and dining room," she said. "Have more of an open concept."

"An open wallet's more like it," Jack said. "My wallet." He stomped over to the refrigerator—new, stainless steel, and very expensive—and looked inside. What was the good of having a top-of-the-line refrigerator if there wasn't anything worth eating inside it? "We never have anything good to eat in this house," Jack said.

Becky rolled her eyes. "I had a fruit smoothie for dinner. I'd be happy to make you one, too."

"That's not food," Jack growled. "Food is something you can chew."

Becky got up from the table and started selecting fruit from the fruit bowl. "Hon, I know you'd love to eat a big, juicy steak every night, but the doctor says it's bad for your cholesterol and blood pressure. A fruit smoothie with protein powder is much healthier. And besides, it wouldn't hurt you to go down a pants size."

Jack's head was pounding with both hunger and anger. "Nothing is ever good enough for you, is it? Everything always has to be improved. The house, your wardrobe, my waistline—everything always has to be upgraded again and again."

Becky was dropping blueberries into the blender. "Well, in the case of your waistline, it would be more of a downgrade that's needed." She smiled at him.

It was the same smile he used to find radiant, but paired with tonight's criticism, it was just annoying.

"That's not funny!" Jack said. "Stop making that smoothie. I don't want a smoothie! I'm going out for a hamburger!"

"But your cholesterol—"

"If I die from cholesterol, at least I'll die full and happy!" Jack said. He stormed out of the house, then realized he'd forgotten his shoes and had to tiptoe back in to get them. It wasn't the dramatic exit he'd been hoping for.

Jack pulled up to the drive-thru at the Golden Heifer.

"Thank you for choosing Golden Heifer. Order when you're ready," the voice on the speaker said.

"Give me the Moo'n'Oink Double Bacon Cheeseburger, a large fry, and a peanut butter shake," Jack said.

"That'll be nine twenty-five. Please pull up to the window," the voice said.

Jack shoved a ten at the young cashier in the window and grabbed his order. He pulled into an empty parking space to eat his meal. When he unwrapped

his burger, there was no bacon on it. Enraged, he got
out of the car and stomped up to the drive-thru window, holding the burger in his hand as evidence.

The cashier, a petite young woman with mousy-
brown hair, said, "I'm sorry, sir, but the drive-thru is
for cars only. If you need to speak to someone, you
need to go inside the restaurant."

"I ordered the Moo'n'Oink Double Bacon
Cheeseburger, and you left out the Oink!" Jack
yelled. "I am not going inside the restaurant. I am
standing here until you make my order right. I
demand bacon!"

The cashier, who was probably still in high school,
looked nervous. "Our company policy is no customers on foot at the drive-thru—"

"I don't give a plugged nickel for what your
company's policy is. I am standing here until I get
what I paid good money for."

"So," the cashier said with a quiver in her voice,
"there was no bacon on your burger?"

"That's what I said," Jack thundered. "Do you not
speak English, or are you just an idiot?"

"I'm sorry you're frustrated, sir," the cashier said.
"I'm going to fix the problem for you. But you have
to understand I'm new at this job. Today's my first
day."

"And if you worked for me, it would be your last,"
Jack said. The young woman looked like she was

near tears, which Jack found strangely satisfying.

Once his order was finally corrected, Jack stomped back to his car and gobbled down the food like a starving dog. A smoothie was not dinner. He was a man, and men needed to *eat*.

He knew he was consuming thousands of calories, but once the food was all gone, he still felt empty.

He reached into the glove compartment and pulled out the bank statement that had come earlier in the day. Jack had a master's degree in business and was an expert number cruncher. But no matter how he crunched them, these numbers were bad.

It shouldn't be this way. Many years ago, when he was in college, Jack had envisioned himself on Wall Street as a real mover and shaker in the world of finance. When that hadn't panned out, he had gotten a job at a bank and started to move his way up the ranks. He worked there several years and his career had been on the rise. Until he had butted heads with his superiors and yelled at his subordinates one too many times and gotten himself fired.

"You're great with numbers, Jack," his old boss had said, "but you're terrible with people."

Hard to get along with, they had said. *Authoritarian personality*, they had said.

Jack had figured that if he built his own business, he wouldn't have to be bossed around by anybody. When the pizza restaurant building had gone up for sale, he took the plunge. He knew that kind of restaurant had been a big hit in other cities, so he figured he couldn't fail.

He was wrong.

He frowned at the numbers on the bank statement. You didn't have to be an expert number cruncher to see that he owed more than he was earning.

In Jack's pocket, his phone—the latest model, which Becky had bought him for *his* birthday with *his* money—rang.

"Hi, Dad." It was Tyson, his son, calling from college.

Jack felt his dark mood lift a bit as he thought back to Tyson's childhood, the ball games and the birthday parties. Things had been happier then. "Hey, buddy, what's up?"

"Uh, well, I just wanted to let you know that I had to use your credit card for a couple of things today." Tyson's voice sounded tense. "One of my classes has an additional textbook I didn't know I needed, and then . . ."

Tyson paused. That pause made Jack nervous.

"And then . . . ?" Jack prompted.

"I had a little oopsie with the car that ended up costing nine hundred dollars. I'm sorry, Dad."

"Nine hundred dollars is a big oopsie! A gigantic oopsie, in fact." Jack felt his face heat up with anger.

a cool evening breeze. He couldn't feel the hugs of friendship or the kisses of love.

Sylvester could walk and talk like a man, but he wasn't fooling anybody, least of all himself. A wooden man was no man at all.

More than anything, Sylvester longed to be real.

Today was the day. Porter had arrived at work early to set up the Puppet Carver on the stage. He had even gone to the office supply store and gotten a flip chart so he could explain how the machine worked in an official-looking way. He wanted everything to be as professional as possible. It had to be, if he was going to save the restaurant and everybody's jobs.

Sage helped him center the puppet carver on the stage. "You've really gone all out, haven't you?" Sage said, looking at the flip chart, then at the uncharacteristic jacket and tie Porter was wearing.

"Yep," Porter said. "I'm a nervous wreck, too. I really need this to go well. I feel like we all need it."

"Yeah, but no pressure, right?" Sage said. "Even though our futures are all in your hands."

Angie came in for her shift and looked up at the stage. "Hey, looking snazzy!" she said to Porter.

"Just trying to make a good impression," Porter said. He tugged at the uncomfortable tie. He had always thought it strange that hanging a strip of cloth from your neck was supposed to make you seem all businesslike and professional. Who had decided that anyway?

Angie flashed him a thumbs-up. "Well, I for one am impressed."

"Wait till you see the machine work," Porter said. "Then you'll be really impressed."

Jack stomped into the dining area, his face already set in a scowl. Clearly he was in a terrible mood. But what else was new?

"Oh, that's right," Jack said, looking up at Porter who was onstage with his invention. "Today's the day you're going to waste my time with that contraption you made."

"Sir, with all due respect, I don't think you'll find it a waste of time," Sage said. "When Porter showed it to me, I thought it was amazing."

"Yeah, well, you're the one who's always working on that 'novel,'" Jack said, using exaggerated finger quotes. "Show me a fiction writer, and I'll show you a liar."

Sage opened his mouth, but before he could put his foot in it, Porter jumped in. "Why don't we go ahead and get to the demonstration? Sage, can you get Edwin out of the kitchen? He wanted to see this, too." Porter hoped having a small errand to run would distract Sage from the fact that Jack had just insulted him.

Soon Edwin, Angie, and Sage were sitting at the

table nearest the stage, smiling and cheering Porter on. Jack sat at a table in the rear and leaned back with his arms crossed over his chest. "Okay," he said. "Impress me."

"Yes, sir!" Porter said. He tried to sound confident even though he was nervous. "Sage, can you give me a hand with this log?"

Sage stepped up and helped him feed the large piece of wood into the machine's opening.

"I've got it from here. Thanks, buddy," Porter said, and Sage took his place back at the table.

"Now, I just push this button, and we watch the magic!" Porter said. After he pushed the button, he stepped aside so everybody could have a clear view of the machine.

Porter could tell right away that something was wrong. The machine was shaking too much and making a strange sputtering sound. There was an unfamiliar rattle from deep within its core. Porter caught Sage's eye and could tell that Sage knew, too.

Porter knew that he had correctly secured the log inside the compartment, but when he opened the door, the machine spat splinters and sawdust so forcefully that it sprayed from the stage into the dining area. Sage and Edwin and Angie were pelted with the stuff.

Angie screamed and shielded her face.

Edwin started sneezing.

Sage ran up on the stage. "Maybe you should turn it off, man," he said.

Porter realized he had been frozen in horror. He quickly touched the button and the machine sputtered to a stop. He looked at the pile of shavings and sawdust in the compartment, and then, fearfully, he looked at Jack.

Jack's face was a mask of rage. His lips were pressed together in a tight line. Porter knew that when those lips parted, whatever came out of them was going to be bad.

It was. What came out first was not even words but the roar of a lion furious to discover it has been caged. He pounded the table with his fists. Finally, the words came. "You absolute idiot! Is this some kind of a sick joke?"

"No, sir," Porter said. He was shaking and sweating profusely. "Something must have malfunctioned this time. It was working great before. You can ask Sage—"

"Sage the liar?" Jack asked, his words dripping venom.

No matter how terrified he was, Porter wasn't going to let Jack talk about his best friend like that. "Sir, Sage isn't—"

"Don't argue with me!" Jack yelled. "You all seem to have forgotten who's in charge here." He stood up from the table. He looked at Porter, then at Angie,

Sage, and Edwin in turn. The look on his face was one of sheer disgust. "I can't imagine there's a business owner in the world with a sorrier group of employees. Lazy, *incompetent*"—he looked at the machine and the mess of shavings and sawdust— "destructive! No wonder this business is in the toilet. I'll go down with my ship like a good captain should, but I know who's to blame for it: the crew. I've got half a mind to fire you all here and now, but we open in thirty minutes, and look at this place. Clean it up, people!"

He stomped back to his office and slammed the door.

"Jack sure was mixing his metaphors there," Sage said. "I'm confused. Are we on a ship or in a toilet?"

Angie shook her head. "I don't know how you can joke at a time like this. We're all going to get fired."

"Oh, I don't think he'll fire us," Edwin said. "He won't want to hire and train new people, not with the business going under. We'll just lose our jobs when the restaurant closes."

"Is that supposed to be good news?" Angie asked.

Porter sat down with his friends at the table. They were the saddest looking bunch he had ever seen, and he couldn't help but feel it was all his fault. "I'm sorry," Porter said. "I don't know what happened, but I do know I let you all down."

"It's okay," Sage said. "All inventors learn from

trial and error. Today was the error part. There will be better days." Sage rose to his feet. "Let me go get some supplies to clean this up."

Together, they swept the stage and wiped down the sawdust-covered tables. They used the giant wet-dry vac to suck up all the shavings off the carpet. Porter and Sage carried the failed machine back to its place in the storage room. Porter was desperate to look inside it and troubleshoot, but he knew that if he hoped to end his night still employed, he needed to focus on one thing: following Jack's orders to the letter, no matter how demanding or ridiculous they were. He and Porter returned to the stage and mopped up the dusty residue.

By opening time, all evidence of the disaster was gone. Jack emerged from his office and surveyed the dining area.

"See?" Porter said. "Spotless. You can't even tell what happened."

"It'll do," Jack said. He took two steps closer to Porter so he was standing right in his face. "That dangerous piece of equipment you're responsible for could have destroyed my whole restaurant." He pointed his index finger at Porter. "You're fired. The rest of you, too. Get out. Now."

"So you make us clean up like we're going to be opening and then you fire us?" Sage said, confused and hurt.

Jack grinned through his rage. "You see, unlike you all, I'm not a fool. I knew if I fired you, then asked you to clean up, the place would still be dirty."

from **The Puppet Carver**
by Sage Brantley

Sylvester knew that he could feel now because he had felt pain beyond imagining. After he had paid the Fixer in money and promises he didn't look forward to keeping, the Fixer had connected Sylvester to the machinery, and pain had shot through his body with the force of electricity as every new nerve, muscle, bone, and tendon in his body were shocked to life. The pain was so strong, he seemed to be able to see it, even hear it, as its intensity drowned out the sounds of his own screams.

But since Sylvester had paid the price in pain, now he could feel pleasure, too. As he walked the city streets, he could feel fresh air in his new lungs. He crossed the street, went into the park, and touched the bark of a tree. Hard, rough. He stopped at an ice-cream truck and bought a cone just so he could touch his lips to its coldness. A lady walked by with a fluffy white dog on a leash.

"Excuse me . . . could I please pet your dog?" Sylvester asked her.

The lady smiled. "Sure. Sophie loves everybody."

Sylvester knelt down and buried his newly sensate hands in the dog's fluffy coat. Tears sprang to his eyes. Now he knew what "soft" meant.

"Thank you," Sylvester said to the dog's owner.

The woman looked at him strangely. She said, "You're welcome," but quickly walked away.

Sylvester looked down at his hands. They felt alive. For the first time since his creation, he felt alive. His hands itched and burned in desperation. All he could think about was what he wanted to touch next.

Jack sat alone in his office, looking at the evening's few receipts. The only good thing about his situation was that he'd finally fired his idiot employees, so he could at least wallow in his misery in peace. He knew if he went home, Becky would want to talk to him about whatever new ways she had found to spend the money that they didn't have.

He knew he should have a talk with Becky about finances, but he couldn't bring himself to do it yet. Becky had married him in part because he was a "good catch" with a promising future. How could he tell her he hadn't made good on that promise? Would she even stay with him if the money ran out? This was a woman who grew up with a mother telling her, "It's just as easy to love a rich man as a poor man," and who had jokingly suggested that the words *for poorer* be struck from their wedding vows.

Tick. Tick.

What was that noise? Jack didn't know if it had been going on a while without him noticing or if it has just started. Either way, now that he had heard it, he couldn't stop hearing it.

Tick. Tick.

It sounded like an especially loud watch. Or a ticking time bomb. Had somebody planted a bomb in the restaurant? If they had, it was a blessing. Jack tried to turn his attention back to his bookkeeping, but the noise was too distracting.

Tick. Tick.

It was more than distracting; it was maddening. What was that Edgar Allan Poe story Jack had read in high school, where the guy kills the old man and then is driven crazy by the nonstop beating sound of the old man's heart? It was like that.

Tick. Tick.

The sound seemed to be coming from behind the stage. Maybe it had something to do with one of the animatronics? Well, there was no way to get any work done with this sound rattling around in his brain. He might as well try to find the source and see if he could make it stop.

Tick. Tick.

The sound was louder when he was on the stage, so he was definitely getting warmer.

He went backstage to the storage room.

TICK. TICK.

The sound was much louder now. It seemed to be coming from the back of the room behind an old dusty curtain one of his idiot employees had hung up for some reason. He pulled back the curtain.

TICK. TICK.

The sound was much louder now, unbearably loud. Jack clamped his hands over his ears. He looked at the disabled animatronics lined up like figures in a wax museum. They weren't where the noise was coming from.

TICK. TICK.

It was coming from the contraption, the horrible mechanical abomination that fool Porter had made. The ticking sound, clearly coming from deep inside the machine's bowels, was making it shake so hard it seemed in danger of falling over. Jack pushed the button on the outside, but nothing happened.

He opened the door, and the sound grew so loud he was sure it could be heard from outside the building.

TICK. TICK. TICK. TICK.

There was some type of control panel inside the machine. Maybe if he just stepped in for a moment, he could find the right button to make the horrible ticking stop.

He stepped inside. It was a tight space. Jack hated tight spaces.

The door slid shut with a *click*. He reached out to open it, but there was no handle on the inside. He thought of banging on the door and yelling, but there was no one there to hear him. And even if there were, there was no way he could be heard over the horrible ticking, which was now so loud it felt like it was coming from inside his own skull.

But then the ticking was drowned out by the whirring of machinery. The contraption appeared to have turned on. He looked at the walls of the machine. They were lined with circular blades that had started to spin and were now extending from the walls toward his body.

What was it that idiot had called this machine? The Puppet Carver.

Jack's heart pounded in terror. He was going to be carved. There was no way to escape.

All around him, the sharp metal blades reached toward his body, less than an inch from making contact with his arms, his legs, his face.

This was it. He was going to die. And painfully. How long would it take, he wondered, for someone to find his body? No one would think to look for him here. Not until there was a smell.

Jack shut his eyes and prepared for the worst.

BANG.

He gasped, startled by the deafening noise.

The loud bang was followed by a cloud of black smoke that filled the small space where Jack was trapped. There was a smell of ozone. He coughed and wondered if he would asphyxiate before the blades in the machine had time to shred him.

Wait. The blades.

The blades had stopped spinning. The machine was quiet. It must have malfunctioned in some way.

The door slid open, releasing the smoke from the compartment. The machine made a sad sputtering noise, and then was still.

Jack was alive! He couldn't believe it. He stepped out of the compartment like he was stepping into a new, better world. He looked himself over. No harm done, not to him anyway. The Puppet Carver might be broken beyond repair, but it hadn't really worked right in the first place.

Jack felt himself smiling. When was the last time he had smiled genuinely? He couldn't even remember. But now, back from the cliff's edge of death, there seemed to be so many reasons to smile. The problems that had consumed him before didn't seem as important. Money didn't matter that much. All that mattered was that he was alive.

Jack walked out of the building. He looked up at the night sky. The stars sparkled, and the moon blanketed the world in a silver glow. It was so beautiful that tears sprang to his eyes. When was the last time he had really seen the moon and stars? When was the last time he had cried?

Looking back at the last decade of his life, the only feelings he could remember were anger and fear.

Anger at his employees, at his wife, at his son. Fear of losing money, power, status. What kind of a life was that?

Well, that stopped now. It was a new day. Well . . . a new night anyway. He was going to be nicer to his wife, to his son, to his employees, to the random people he transacted with in day-to-day life. Jack felt his heart brimming with love and kindness. He was like Ebenezer Scrooge in *A Christmas Carol* after his encounter with the ghosts, no longer a mean old miser but a man who could find the goodness in life and people and even within himself.

Jack got in his car. How fortunate he was to have such a nice car. How fortunate he was to have a car at all! Many people were not so lucky. He started the car and headed toward home. He hoped Becky was still awake. He had a lot to say to her.

"Oh!" he said as he drove by the Golden Heifer. He turned back to the restaurant and pulled into the drive-thru line. When it was his turn, the voice on the intercom said, "Thank you for choosing Golden Heifer. Please order when you're ready."

"Actually, I have a question to ask you," Jack said.

"Yes," the voice said.

"Are you the young lady who was working the drive-thru Tuesday night?" he asked.

"Um . . . yes, sir." She sounded uncomfortable.

"Good. I've got something I need to say to you. I'll just pull up to the window, okay?"

"Uh . . . would you like to speak to the manager?"

"No. My beef is with you." Jack laughed. "Get it? Beef? Because you sell hamburgers." He couldn't tell if the drive-thru worker thought this was funny or not.

When he pulled up to the window, the young woman said, "Oh. You."

"Yes, me," Jack said. "But I'm a very different me than I was last night. I wanted to apologize for my behavior. You were learning a new job, and you were doing your best and being very polite, and I was rude. I'm sorry."

"Thank you?" the young woman said, but her inflection rose as if she were asking a question. Clearly, she was finding this encounter puzzling.

"Thank *you*," Jack said, "for your politeness and understanding." He sat there and smiled at her.

"You're welcome." The young woman looked at the line of cars growing behind Jack's vehicle. "Did you want to order anything, sir?" she asked.

"No, I'm good." He found himself chuckling. "I'm really, really good. You have a nice night now."

"You too."

Jack drove away, feeling the weight of one of his regrets lifting. But fixing one isolated incident like a drive-thru dustup was easy. With Becky, with Tyson, there were years of bad behavior on his part, way more than he could fix with a simple *I'm sorry*.

An idea popped into Jack's head. *Doughnuts. Doughnuts would be a start.*

Back when he and Becky had been young and broke, they used to meet for dates at the Dunky Doughman, an all-night doughnut place near the copy shop where Becky had been working at the time. Despite its stupid name, the Dunky Doughman was the perfect place for a cheap date. The two of them would scrape up enough money for a doughnut each—chocolate frosted for Becky and maple frosted for Jack—and two cups of coffee. The manager didn't mind that they only spent five dollars and took up a booth for hours, talking and drinking cup after cup of coffee. Or if he did, he never said anything.

That was back when he and Becky really talked to each other. Before the money, before parenthood, before all the stresses of responsible adult life. They talked earnestly about their dreams, their goals, their future. If Jack brought home doughnuts from the Dunky Doughman, maybe it would remind her of those conversations. Maybe it would be the first step toward getting them talking again.

There was no street parking near the doughnut shop, so Jack had to use the parking garage a block away. He wasn't thrilled by this fact; really, the

Dunky Doughman wasn't in the safest neighborhood to be wandering at night. But he had become increasingly convinced that showing up with a bag of doughnuts might be the path back to Becky's heart. It was a thoughtful gesture, and it had been a long time since he had been thoughtful.

Jack didn't like parking garages. There was something eerie about the flickering fluorescent lighting and the way sounds echoed. The elevators always seemed to be on the verge of breaking and were infested by foul and mysterious odors.

Jack breathed a sigh of relief when the elevator doors opened. He hustled toward the garage's exit. At first he heard only the sound of his own shuffling footsteps. But then he was sure he heard another pair of footsteps behind him. He casually glanced over his shoulder. There was no need to be afraid. It was probably just some regular person on a regular errand like he was.

But Jack saw no one.

He chalked it up to the weird echo effect of the parking garage and walked through the exit onto the street. He walked past a dry cleaner's and an insurance office. Most of the businesses on the street were dark and locked up for the night, but in the distance, he could see the light of the Dunky Doughman sign with its smiling doughnut mascot.

He heard the footsteps behind him again. He

turned around but only saw a flash of movement as whoever it was ducked into an alley.

Jack was pretty sure he was just being paranoid; after his near-death experience earlier in the day, it made sense that his nerves were on edge.

He heard the steps again. They sounded wet, squishy, like somebody walking in galoshes in the rain. Jack started walking more quickly, and the steps sped up to match his.

He was tempted to turn around and confront the person, but what good would that do if the person were armed? He broke into a run—though he knew he was too out of shape to run for long. The squishy steps behind him ran, too.

Suddenly the doughnut shop seemed too far away to be a safe destination. He had to go inside somewhere—to find a place with people and lights, a place where his pursuer would not follow him. He caught sight of an office building on the left, tried the door, and found it open. Once inside, he noticed that the door had a chain, which he quickly fastened. There was also a lock on the doorknob, which he turned.

Feeling a little safer, he took a deep breath and turned around to survey the space where he found himself. There were no people, and the only light was from a single bare bulb overhead. The building looked abandoned. Graffiti had been spray-painted all over the walls. The glass in the windows had been smashed, and doors that had once led to offices had been torn off their hinges. He glanced inside one room to see a desk and a broken office chair and piles of garbage, probably from people who had been squatting in the space.

Squatters. There was something else to fear. But the building was as silent as a mausoleum, and he seriously doubted that the potential mugger who had been following him would go to the trouble of trying to unlock the building's front door. For the time being, he was safe. He glanced back at the front door just to confirm that he'd locked it and saw there was movement in the tiny crack between the bottom of the door and the floor.

Something was oozing through the crack. It was some sort of gelatinous substance, and its movement was slow and steady. It was pink, but it was a horrible pink. Not the pink of cake frosting and party balloons.

It was the pink of some living creature's insides.

Jack took a step backward. He knew he needed to move more quickly, but he was transfixed by the sight of whatever was in front of him. Although it had the appearance of some sort of goo, it seemed to be moving under its own power. It wasn't an inanimate substance.

It was alive.

The sudden realization shook Jack out of his trance, and he ran down the hallway. He heard the squishy, sloppy steps behind him again, but he didn't turn around to look. He just kept running. At the end of the hall was a door marked EXIT. He pushed on the door, but it wouldn't budge. Was it locked from the outside? Broken?

He turned around. The thing, whatever it was, was getting closer.

It was a pile of parts he couldn't make sense of— much of it was somewhere between solid and liquid, but there were fully solid parts as well—bundles of long, snakelike tubes; veiny bags and pouches. When Jack was a little boy, he had spent winter break at his grandparents' farm. He remembered watching his grandpa and uncle butcher a hog once. They had hung its body from a tree. His uncle had sliced down the hog's middle, and its guts had spilled out into a bucket with a sickening splat. This thing . . . that was how it sounded when it moved.

Since he had no luck with the exit, Jack tried another nearby door. It was unlocked. He quickly opened it, darted in, and slammed and locked the door behind him. He was inside another ruined office. The floor was strewn with garbage, and the window was cracked, but strangely, a plaque still hung on the wall saying EMPLOYEE OF THE MONTH. An empty bookshelf about the height of Jack's waist had been knocked onto the floor. Jack dragged it to the door and shoved it under the doorknob at an angle.

Winded, Jack sat down in the chair behind the desk. Here he was, looking like the boss he had been for years, but in a ruined office, hiding, in fear for his life.

He should have known the locked door was useless. Long, slimy tendrils were already snaking their way through the cracks underneath it. Pink slime dripped around the sides of the door and pooled onto the floor, merging itself with the creeping tendrils.

Jack looked to the window as a possible escape route, but more of the globby substance was slithering over the windowsill.

Jack looked back at the door, where the thing continued to ooze out. *Is there more than one thing, or is it all the same thing? What is happening?*

There was a loud slurping sound like someone trying to pull their feet out of deep mud. Rapidly, so fast he couldn't even make sense of it, the mass of slime and solids reconstituted itself into an upright being that sat in the chair across the desk from Jack.

The thing had approximations of arms and legs and a lumpy mound that stood in for a head. It was made of the translucent pink goo, under which its organs were visible. Somehow it reminded Jack of the awful gelatin salad his mom used to make, with canned fruit suspended under the slimy surface.

It had no mouth or nose, but it had eyes. Dark eyes that stared at Jack as though the thing could see into him the way he could see into it.

"What . . . what do you want?" Jack asked, his voice trembling. He didn't want to die, not when he had just had one near miss, not when he was just remembering what was important.

The creature kept looking at him. Then, slowly, it raised one arm and reached toward him. Like elastic, its arm stretched, growing thinner as it reached across the length of the desk to touch Jack's face.

Pain like Jack had never known shot through him. But it wasn't physical pain. He felt the pain of hurt, neglect, abuse. It was the pain of every employee he had ever yelled at or fired, the pain of his son every time he had missed one of his ball games or unfairly criticized him, the pain of his wife for every forgotten birthday or unkind word. Jack was filled with all the emotional pain he had ever caused, and it was more intense than he could bear. He doubled over and squeezed his tear-filled eyes shut, sure he was about to die from a real broken heart.

But then the pain left him just as suddenly as it had come, and he was awash in an overwhelming sense of relief. When he opened his eyes, the creature was gone.

Becky was in bed but awake, watching one of her shows about home remodeling on TV.

"Hiya, Becks," Jack said, pleased to hear his old pet name for her come out of his mouth. He sat down on the bed next to her. "Can I talk to you for a few minutes?"

"Sure." She aimed the remote and switched off the TV. "Is everything okay? You're not sick or anything, are you?" Her brow furrowed like it did when she was worried.

"No, it's nothing like that."

"Good . . . I mean, it's just been a really long time since you seemed like you wanted to talk to me, so I was afraid it was going to be something bad."

"It is bad, but you've done nothing wrong. I wanted to say . . . I know I've been a bad husband lately, and I'm sorry." *Lately* didn't begin to cover it, he knew. He couldn't remember the last time he'd acted like a decent husband. Maybe when Tyson was little?

"Wow." There were tears in her eyes, which she wiped away. "I wasn't expecting that."

"Well, from now on, you can expect better of me. You can *demand* better of me." He felt his eyes getting a little teary, too. "Part of the reason I've been so on edge is money. The business isn't doing well, Becks. The animatronics keep breaking. Families aren't showing up. I'm losing all this money on food. I don't know how much longer the Pizza Playground can limp along."

Becky took his hand and held it. It had been a long time since she had done that. "Oh, honey, you should've told me. And here I've been yammering away about remodeling and all this stuff that costs a lot of money. I never would've even suggested it if I'd known you'd been worried about money. From now on you've got to promise to tell me when something's wrong."

Jack nodded. "I will. I promise."

"And I promise I'll do the same." She looked him in the eyes. "Actually, you know, I think the reason I've obsessed over the house so much is that I've been sad ever since Tyson left home. Fixing up things in the house distracted me from how much I miss him."

"I miss him, too," Jack said.

"Nobody tells you how hard it's going to be when your kid goes off to college." Becky wiped another tear away. "They act like it's one big party, but it's not. Actually, I've been thinking I might go back to work. There's an opening at my old real estate office, and they called to ask if I was interested. I figure that way I could keep my mind active and see other people during the day." She squeezed his hand. "Plus, if I got a job, we'd have two incomes instead of one. It might ease some of your financial worries."

Jack tucked a lock of hair behind her ear. "If that's really what you want to do, then I support you." Back before Tyson was born, Becky had been a successful real estate agent. He had to admit that the thought of someone else in the family earning money was comforting.

"It's really what I want to do." She smiled. "There's no need to be a stay-at-home mom when there's no kid staying at home anymore. It was either get a job or get a dog to turn into my surrogate child."

"I think you made the right choice," Jack said, smiling in return. "Say, do you think Tyson's still up?"

"It's not even eleven, and he's a college student," Becky said. "*Of course* he's still up. For him, the night is young." She snuggled down under the covers. "But it's past my bedtime."

"Mine, too," Jack agreed. "But all the same, I want to give Tyson a call."

Jack took his phone into the kitchen and poured himself a glass of water. Tyson answered on the first ring, but he sounded low.

"Hey, buddy," Jack said. "I just wanted to check in to see how you're doing."

"I promise I haven't spent any more of your money if that's what you want to know."

"No, I wasn't calling about money. I was calling about you."

"Really?" Tyson's tone had a hard edge. "Because when we talked earlier this week, you wouldn't even let me tell you about the car emergency I had. You were too upset that I had charged your credit card nine hundred dollars to make the repairs."

Jack felt a little tug at his heart. Was what Tyson saying true? Could Jack have really been so cold? "I'm sorry if that's how I seemed. You didn't have an accident, did you?"

"No, but I could have easily. My car broke a belt on the interstate and just stopped dead. It was a miracle I didn't get hit. All these cars were just whizzing past me, and I was right int the center lane. Finally, a police officer helped me get the car moved to the side of the road and called a tow truck. I was really scared, Dad." His voice broke with emotion.

"Anybody would've been scared in that situation, son." Jack felt the full weight of guilt bearing down on him. "I'm just glad you're okay. Did the mechanic get the car fixed okay?"

"Yeah, it's running great now."

"Good." Jack knew that the mechanic had overcharged Tyson, taking advantage of the fact that Tyson was an inexperienced boy who didn't know what a fair price was.

But the important thing was that Tyson was safe. You couldn't put a price on that.

"Listen, buddy, I'm gonna let you go," Jack said. "I'm sure you've got way more interesting things to do than to talk to your old man. If you need anything, let me know, okay? I love you, buddy."

"I love you, too, Dad," Tyson said, sounding confused.

As soon as Jack ended the call, he sipped his water and ate one of Becky's delicious homemade oatmeal cranberry pecan cookies. In the morning, he thought, he would make some phone calls. He would tell the kids he'd fired—because that's what they were, just kids—to come back to work as usual. He would make things right with them.

Jack climbed the stairs, put on his pajamas, and brushed his teeth. He slid into the cool, clean sheets beside Becky, who was already asleep. As soon as Jack closed his eyes, so was he. It was a deep, peaceful rest.

Porter didn't have much of an appetite, but he nibbled his toast and sipped his coffee. He couldn't face the two sunny-side up eggs on his plate and wasn't sure why he had ordered them, except out of habit. It felt like the eggs were staring at him judgmentally.

He knew that what was bothering him was the same thing that was bothering everybody else in their booth in the Golden Heifer, where they were having their traditional late-Saturday-morning breakfast: They had all received the call from Jack, all agreed to report back to work at the Pizza Playground, but they were fearful about what might happen when they got there.

Angie was toying with her pancakes. "So on a

scale of one to ten, how bad a mood do you think Jack will be in today?"

"An eleven. Definitely an eleven," Sage said, picking at his fruit plate.

"I've got a job interview at that fancy new steakhouse on Monday," Edwin said. "They're still hiring, I'm just sayin'."

"I don't think I'd ever get hired as a server someplace fancy," Angie said. "I'm not ladylike enough, you know?" She crammed a whole strip of bacon in her mouth, as if to illustrate her point. "I'm doomed to sling pizzas at preschoolers."

"Yeah, I don't guess the fancy steakhouse has animatronics they need somebody to service," Porter threw in.

"Yeah," Sage said, laughing, "but wouldn't it be weird if they did? There'd be all these rich adults eating steak and lobster and singing 'Head, Shoulders, Knees, and Toes' along with Baron von Bear and his friends."

Edwin smiled at Sage and shook his head. "You are weird, man. But they're hiring cleaning staff for the night shift. You ought to apply. Fancy places need their bathrooms cleaned just like regular places."

"That's encouraging to hear," Sage said. "You know me, student and novelist by day, toilet scrubber by night."

They paid their bill and walked together to the

Pizza Playground with all the enthusiasm of condemned prisoners.

When they reached the building, they saw the outside had been decorated with dozens of brightly colored balloons. A sign read, *Special Today: Large Cheese Pizza, Four Drinks, for $10—includes 25 FREE game tokens!*

Porter couldn't imagine Jack ever voluntarily giving away anything for free. "That's actually a pretty good deal," he said.

Apparently other people thought so, too. A family of four paused and looked at the sign. The dad reached into his wallet, pulled out a ten-dollar bill, and said, "Why not?"

The family went inside.

"Wow," Porter said, "I feel almost hopeful."

Sage wasn't as enthused. "Be careful. Remember that Jack has given us plenty of reasons to be pessimistic."

Porter had to admit that Sage was right.

They entered the dining area. Jack was standing next to the table with the family who had just come in and was chatting with them as he filled their glasses and set the pitcher with the rest of the soda on the table. Porter was shocked to see Jack pleasantly interacting with—and actually waiting on—customers.

"Did you see that?" Angie whispered to Porter

and Sage. "Since when does Jack hand out free refills without customers practically begging for them?"

"Since now, apparently," Porter said. "And look at his face. What is he doing?"

Sage was similarly in shock. "I think . . . he's smiling."

Seeing Jack smile was like seeing a dog dancing on its hind legs. It wasn't physically impossible, but it seemed highly unlikely.

"There's my stellar staff!" Jack said, giving them a friendly wave. "Edwin, would you be willing to go into the kitchen and make these fine folks one of your delicious pizzas?"

"Sure," Edwin said, looking at Jack like he had just sprouted an extra head.

"Angie, Sage, Porter, how are you guys doing today?" Jack said, grinning at them. "It's getting close to final exams, isn't it? Are you studying hard?"

Porter looked over at his equally confused friends. "Y-yes, sir."

"That's good," Jack said. "I'm proud of you."

"Thank you, sir."

Jack grinned warmly at the trio, taking them aside. "I do hope that all of you will accept my apologies for my behavior yeterday. I also hope you'll accept a two-dollar-an-hour raise." He gave Porter a chuck on the shoulder. "And what's with all this 'sir' stuff? There's no need for formality. This is

Pizza Playground. We're here to have fun!"

Porter and Sage shared a look. In the past, Jack had always demanded that his employees call him "sir," as if he were their drill sergeant in boot camp.

Another family of four came in, perhaps also lured by the ten-dollar special. "Welcome, welcome!" Jack called, like an enthusiastic game show host. "Who's ready for pizza, games, and a show?"

All the kids cheered while their parents smiled down at them.

Angie seated the new family and took their drink orders. Porter went behind the stage to make sure that the animatronics and sound system were in good working order. On the other side of the curtain, he could hear children talking and laughing, the games in the arcade beeping and blipping. He wasn't sure what had caused the change, but whatever it was, Pizza Playground had started to feel like what it was supposed to: A place for families to have fun. A place where the employees helped create an atmosphere of entertainment and even enjoyed themselves in the process.

But how could the place have felt so bad yesterday and feel the opposite today? How could Jack have fired the whole staff yesterday, then rehired them and showered them with kind words and a raise today? It didn't make any sense.

Porter remembered something his mom used to

say: "When good luck happens, don't question it."

It was sound advice.

He programmed the show to start. He stepped backstage so he wouldn't be seen by the audience. The canned music started to play, and the sparkly red curtain parted to reveal the two patched-together, barely moving animatronic figures—the bear and the weird bird thing—that now made up the "house band."

Even with just two "performers" on the stage, the kids in the audience screamed like rabid fans at a music festival.

Porter chuckled. It was nice that they were enjoying the fruits of his labor. *Later tonight*, he thought, *I should tinker around some more with the Puppet Carver and see if I can figure out what went wrong. Maybe if I can get it fixed and, if Jack's still in a good mood, he'll be willing to watch another demonstration. A successful one this time.*

The ten-dollar special had been a success. Families had trickled in over the course of the night to take advantage of the cheap dinner offer, and business, though not booming, had been steady. Jack felt encouraged. No, he felt more than encouraged. He felt great.

Tonight, as he looked around the restaurant, he saw not a doomed money pit but a place full of possibilities. He just had to think harder about ways to bring people in, and tonight had been evidence that when he put his brain to use and tried something new, his efforts would be rewarded. Making the place a success was a challenge, but it was a challenge he could rise to.

One reason he could rise to the challenge was because of his great employees, but in order to ensure their loyalty, he had to let them know that he appreciated them.

Porter and Angie were wiping down the tables in the dining area, and Sage was mopping the floor. They were all such hard workers. He knew Edwin was working equally hard cleaning up the kitchen. Once the money was rolling in better, Jack thought, he should hire a dishwasher to help Edwin out in the kitchen. When business was booming—and Jack felt sure that it would be soon—one guy in the kitchen wouldn't be enough.

"Hey, are you guys doing anything special after you get out of here?" Jack asked.

Angie looked at Porter and Sage, who shrugged. "Just studying, probably."

"Well, if you guys can stick around for a little bit after closing, I thought I might order some Chinese takeout. My treat. No need to study on an empty stomach, right?"

Angie smiled warily. "Sure, Jack. Thanks."

It was strange. When Jack was kind to them, they

seemed suspicious, like they didn't trust him, like there had to be a catch. Well, he was just going to have to work harder to earn their trust.

Jack sat crowded around a table with Porter, Sage, Angie, and Edwin. They passed around little white boxes containing rice, lo mein, Mongolian beef, and moo goo gai pan.

"This was really nice of you, Jack," Angie said, messily picking up some noodles with her chopsticks.

"It sure beats leftover pizza," Edwin added.

"That's the truth," Porter said. "No offense to your pizza cooking skills, Edwin."

Edwin smiled. "None taken. I probably get sicker of it than the rest of you since I'm cooking it AND eating it."

"You've been really nice all day today," Sage said. He looked at Jack with a strange intensity. "It's like you're a new man."

Jack smiled, happy to be at a table full of happy people sharing good food. It felt like a holiday, a celebration. It was the way things should be. He wasn't sure why things felt so different, so much better, but they did.

Jack really was a new man.

from **The Puppet Carver**
by Sage Brantley
   Sylvester held his newborn daughter in his arms. With

one hand, he touched her impossibly soft cheek. His eyes filled with tears at the same time his lips spread into a smile. This, *he thought*. This was what it meant to be human.
   THE END

Sage couldn't believe it. The novel was finished. As he walked backstage to the storage room, he read and reread the novel's last line, smiling to himself.

Sage would never admit it to anyone, but he was so moved by the beauty of his novel that there were tears in his eyes. It had taken him so many long nights of writing and rewriting, of sacrificing sleep and time with friends. Finally, he was completely satisfied with his work and hoped that soon a publisher would be, too. And then it would be goodbye, Pizza Playground, and hello, bestseller list! He laughed out loud. He knew he was being ridiculously optimistic, but why not? It could happen.

He just needed to do a favor for a friend, and then he could go home to celebrate. Sage pulled back the glittery purple curtain.

There it was. The Puppet Carver, named in honor of his novel.

Porter had told Sage he was going to have to go back to the drawing board and develop what would hopefully be a more effective Puppet Carver 2.0. The old machine would have to be scrapped, but

Porter said he didn't have the heart to do it himself. Sage had promised that he would take care of it.

Sage wrestled with the machine, trying to figure out the best way to get it outside to the dumpster. As he tugged on it, he became aware of a slight sloshing sound.

And then there was the smell. A rotting, fetid smell that made him gag. It seemed to be coming from the bottom of the machine. Maybe a rat had crawled in there and died or something.

Sage kneeled in front of the Puppet Carver so he could reach the drawer at the bottom that served as a reservoir for all the waste generated during the carving process. "Here we go," he muttered as he prepared for the source of the smell.

When he pulled out the drawer, the smell was so strong that his nose was assaulted. The sight was even worse than the smell—slimy pink entrails and mangled organs. Was that a kidney or a piece of a liver? Not the organs of a rat, but of a much larger creature. Human-size.

Sage had no idea what could have happened here, but it was all the more reason to get the whole thing to the dumpster as fast as possible. Holding his breath, he dumped the contents of the drawer in a garbage bag. They landed with a wet *splat*. He threw the bag in the dumpster and walked away, ready to put his days at the Pizza Playground behind him.

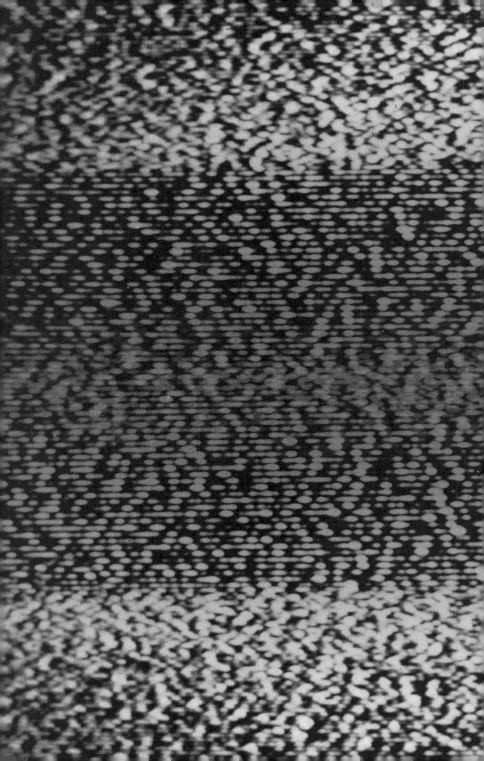

JUMP
FOR
TICKETS

The little kid's grating voice blared through Colton's headphones, as high-pitched and annoying as a smoke alarm. "Did you just kill me? That was harsh, dude!"

"It was a mercy killing, squeaker," Colton said, emphasizing the new deepness of his voice. He was going for a tough and sarcastic tone, like an action hero. "Too bad you can respawn."

Colton hated the little kids who tried to play *Hammer of Odin,* his favorite online role-playing game. The little brats dominated the chat function, trying and failing to make the more mature players think they were cool. *Hammer of Odin* wasn't appropriate for little kids anyway. It was rated *T,* so it was for teens like Colton. The little pip-squeaks should stick to playing *Block Builder* like Colton had played last year when he was still in middle school.

When Colton looked back at middle school, he

didn't even recognize the person he had been. For one thing, his dad was still alive. Colton had been a happy, carefree, regular kid, not worried about anything more serious than how long it would take him to save up his generous allowance for a new video game. But on an icy road just over a year ago, the accident happened, and everything had changed.

Life had changed. Colton had changed.

Colton couldn't get over the unfairness of the accident. His dad had been relatively young and took good care of himself, but none of that mattered because of a stupid patch of ice and a strip of road without a guardrail. When it first happened, Colton had kept all his sadness inside. He hadn't cried, not even at the funeral. But over time, his sadness had hardened into anger. How could a person not be angry living in a world where good people died for

Colton knew that his mom and some of his teach-ers were worried about how cold and bitter he seemed. What was he supposed to do? A happy dance? His dad was dead, and he lived in a world where people rarely got what they deserved. If he lashed out sometimes, so what? He was suffering, and if other people ended up getting a taste of that pain, then at least he didn't suffer alone.

Colton jumped in surprise when a hand touched his shoulder. He looked up to see his mom, dressed in her light blue scrubs. Her curly brown hair was pulled back in a tight bun, like she always wore it when she was going to work. She gestured at him to remove his headset. He sighed in exasperation but reluctantly complied. "What?"

His mom shook her head at him, though she was smiling. "I'm going to work is *what*. I'm pulling an eight-to-eight shift tonight, heaven help me. Here's a ten-dollar bill if you want to go out and get a soda and play some games. That way, at least one of us will be having fun."

"Okay, thanks, Mom." The ten-dollar bill was a once-a-week treat. Once a month, right after payday, she would give him a twenty.

"You've got your key, right?" She put on the lan-yard she kept next to the door.

Colton resisted the urge to roll his eyes. "Yes, Mom."

"Remember to lock the door if you go out," she said, grabbing her keys and purse. "And call the third-floor nurses' station if you need anything. One of the other nurses can come find me."

"I will," Colton said, putting his headset back on to block out the barrage of nagging. After he got to a good stopping place in *Hammer of Odin*, he probably would head over to Freddy Fazbear's. The pizza place was less than a ten-minute walk from their apartment building. He knew he was really too old for Freddy's, and he had no interest in the creepy animatronics or the bland pizza. But some of the games were still fun, and there was the lure of tickets that could be redeemed for prizes.

It took a ridiculous number of tickets to win any-thing good, of course. Most kids—especially the stupid little ones—cashed in their tickets at the end of their visit and walked away with garbage like tiny plastic dinosaurs or a handful of cheap candy. But Colton wasn't shortsighted like those babies. He'd been sav-ing up his tickets for a long time—months—so he could cash them in for something really good. For the astronomical "price" of 10,000 tickets, there was a new handheld game console he had his eye on, which was two models more up-to-date than the one he was currently playing.

That was the thing about living with just his mom. She worked hard at her job as a licensed practical nurse at the hospital, but one income didn't go far. With his dad gone, Colton and his mom had learned to settle for less: living in a small apartment instead of a house, buying store-brand groceries instead of the brand-name stuff, playing older games on older equipment while Colton's friends seemed to buy new games and consoles as casually as if they were bottles of soda. He wasn't a poor kid, exactly—they had a roof over their heads and clothes to wear and plenty to eat—but there was no money for what his mom always called "luxuries." New, name-brand clothes and sneakers were luxuries. So were new games and nearly anything else that had the word *new* in front of it.

Colton understood that his mom couldn't make money magically appear, but maybe if he spent enough time at Freddy's, he could make tickets magically appear. If he got good at the highest ticket-yielding games, he could win that game console. Ten thousand tickets. He was going to do it.

When he had told his mom the plan, she laughed and said, "Remind me never to take you to Las Vegas when you're old enough to gamble."

But winning the tickets at Freddy's wasn't about Las Vegas–style luck. It was about skill—using your abilities to make the system work in your favor.

Colton knew he had the skills.

Colton signed out of *Hammer of Odin*, went to the

kitchen, and made himself a ham-and-cheese sandwich with pickles and mayo, which he gobbled standing over the sink. He had already eaten dinner, but he was always hungry these days. *It's like you have a hollow leg*, his mom always said. He grabbed his jacket and shoved the ten-dollar bill in its pocket. Time to win some tickets.

It always took a few minutes to adjust to how overstimulating the environment at Freddy's was. Multicolored lights flashed, arcade games bleeped and blipped, and a "band" of creepy animatronic animals led by top-hatted Freddy Fazbear "sang" canned versions of kiddie tunes. And then there were the kiddies themselves, laughing, screaming, throwing tantrums, and running around underfoot like cockroaches. It was all Colton could do not to squash them.

Colton took a quick trip by the prize counter to make sure his dream console was still there. It was. There was still hope.

He backtracked to the counter where tokens were sold. He laid down his ten and told the cashier, "Ten dollars in tokens, please." He wasn't going to waste any of his limited funds on a soda—no reason for spending a buck ninety-nine that wouldn't move him any closer to his goal. If he got thirsty, he would drink from the water fountain.

He went to play his regulars, DeeDee's Fishing Hole and BB's Ball Drop, each of which yielded him a fairly long ribbon of tickets. The evening was off to a promising start.

Near the stage, a table full of rug rats—kindergartners, from the looks of them—were munching pizza and wearing stupid-looking paper birthday hats decorated with cartoon characters. Their chubby, blank faces were smeared with pepperoni grease and tomato sauce. As he looked at them, Colton felt actual physical repulsion, as though he was surveying a nest of squirming maggots.

And then Colton saw him. One of the horrible pizza-gobbling goblins was his little cousin Aidan. Aidan was the most annoying little brat of all time, and because he was Colton's aunt Katie's kid, the two of them were forced to spend time in each other's presence on holidays, birthdays, and whenever else his mom and aunt wanted to get together. The worst thing about Aidan was that he loved Colton desperately, and no matter how much venom Colton spewed at him, Aidan only seemed to love him more.

"Please don't let him see me, please don't let him see me," Colton muttered under his breath.

But it was too late. Aidan's gaze was already focused on Colton, and he was smiling and waving frantically. The little boy dropped his pizza slice, got up from the table, and made a beeline for Colton.

Before Colton could protest, Aidan was hugging him. Colton stood stiffly, his arms raised as though a police officer had just told him to freeze. He refused to participate in this hug.

Aidan finally let go. His smile hadn't faded. "Wow, I can't believe I get to go to a birthday party at Freddy's *and* I get to see my cousin at the same time! This is the best night ever!"

"For one of us, maybe," Colton said.

Aidan laughed. "You're funny, Colton! I'd better get back to the party. It's almost time for our favorite game! You know the one, right?" Aidan gave him a little chuck on the arm.

Colton did know what game Aidan was talking about but refused to acknowledge it. He rubbed his arm as if Aidan had injured him.

Thankfully, Aidan ran back to join his putrid pint-size friends.

"Now who's ready to Jump! For! Tickets!" a recorded voice asked as the animatronic Freddy flapped his jaws.

The greasy little brats jumped up and down and cheered. Their high-pitched voices made Colton want to clap his hands over his ears.

"Get ready for the Ticket Pulverizer Countdown!" the recorded Freddy voice ordered.

A bored-looking college-aged girl in a Freddy's uniform opened the door to the Ticket Pulverizer, a game in a sealed transparent booth that could generate an absurd number of tickets. The Ticket Pulverizer usually cost four tokens per person, but for birthday parties, the birthday kid and guests got one visit to the Pulverizer for free. Colton watched as the disinterested-seeming employee unlocked the booth, and the pip-squeaks poured in, giggling and yelling with excitement.

"Now get ready to Jump for Tickets!" the recorded Freddy voice ordered. "And say hello to our friend, Coils the Birthday Clown!"

Colton didn't like clowns, and he especially didn't like this clown. Coils the Birthday Clown animatronic had wonky eyes—one that seemed to look straight ahead while the other veered down and to the right—and a weird, open-jawed grin that reminded Colton of those carnival games where you shoot water in the clown's mouth. Its lanky body was dressed in a lemon-and-lime-colored striped costume that was decorated with little jingly bells, which, Colton guessed, was so you could hear the clown before you saw it. It reminded him of the old story about the mice who want to hang a bell on a cat to use as an early warning system.

The clown's name came from its arms, which were yellow stretchy coils that reminded Colton of the old-fashioned landline phone at his grandmother's house. In one of the clown's three-fingered, white-gloved hands, it held several fanned-out tickets.

"Now, who's ready to Jump! For! Tickets!" the clown's high-pitched voice said again, turning up the drama.

The squeakers went insane.

"Prepare for the Ticket Pulverizer Countdown! Now, when I finish counting, everybody jump up and down as hard as you can, all together. Here we go! Ten, nine, eight, seven, six, five, four, three, two . . . one!" The clown's voice actor had really been trying to turn up the excitement when he recorded this. "Now . . . Jump! For! Tickets!"

Laughing and squealing, the little kids leaped up and then landed in unison, as the parents watching them called, "Jump! Jump! Jump!" With each landing, they pushed down the platform on the floor of the booth, which caused tickets to fall from the ceiling. Delighted, they grabbed the tickets in their greedy little fists.

Colton watched the spectacle with a mixture of jealousy and disgust. All those tickets, and the little brats were wasting them. You only got to keep what you caught, and the little kids were being stupid about it, grabbing over and over with their hands, dropping the tickets they had just caught in order to catch the new ones. They weren't smart enough to stuff the tickets into their pockets, down their shirts, inside their socks. If it were Colton, he'd stick tickets everywhere they'd fit: In his underwear. In his mouth.

But even though the little kids annoyed him, they weren't what really filled him with rage. The true object of his wrath was the Ticket Pulverizer itself. It was rigged to give an unfair advantage to little kids. He knew it. He had watched it dozens of times, maybe even a hundred, and the results were always the same. Whenever there were little kids inside it, jumping and stomping, there was always a veritable blizzard of tickets. If Colton and other teens jumped for tickets, there were only a few flurries. It made no sense. Colton was no physicist, but he knew that heavier, stronger kids generated more force than shrimpy, weak ones. More force should equal more tickets. It was as simple as that.

As Colton watched the pip-squeak party guests exit the Ticket Pulverizer, an idea began to form in his mind. If the Ticket Pulverizer had been rigged to favor little kids, could it be rerigged to favor big ones? Colton excelled at his tech classes in high school, and he liked to hang around his uncle Mike's car repair shop to learn how to fix things. He was good at mechanical stuff.

Now that the kids had cleared out of the Ticket Pulverizer, Colton approached it for a closer look. Getting inside the machine wouldn't be hard. If it was turned on, he would just have to feed it four tokens. He surveyed the booth's bright red platform, which was printed with pictures of child-size footprints. He looked at the screws that connected the platform to the bottom of the booth. Wouldn't tightening those screws make the platform harder to push down? He needed to give it some more thought, but he was confident that he could rerig the Pulverizer so it favored bigger visitors instead of small ones. Justice would be served, and after only a dozen or so rounds of Jump for Tickets, Colton would be able to claim his new game console.

"Hey, Colton!" Aidan's annoying, high-pitched voice interrupted Colton's thoughts.

Colton looked down to see the freckle-faced freak holding so many long ribbons of tickets he could hardly grasp them in his tiny fists.

"Hey, Colton, look how many tickets I got!" Aidan said.

"I see," Colton hissed. "Now shoo."

"Do you want half my tickets?" Aidan asked, holding out a fistful.

"I don't want your stupid tickets. I want you to. Go. Away." Colton was filled with a white-hot rage. Why did this loathsome little creature have to pester him all the time?

"Okay. Bye, Colton." Aidan ran off to join his repulsive little friends.

With Aidan gone, Colton returned to his plan.

It was a beautiful plan. Except for one thing.

Colton suddenly realized that he couldn't dismantle the Ticket Pulverizer when Freddy's was open and full of employees, screaming kids, and exhausted parents. If a worker caught him messing with the machine, the manager would be called, and Colton would be thrown out and maybe even banned from returning. If the manager was in a really bad mood, she might even call the police. Getting in that kind of trouble was a risk he couldn't take.

No. If Colton was going to fix the Ticket Pulverizer, he was going to have to do it when the place was empty.

Colton realized that to get what he wanted, he had only one choice. Late one night, while his mom was at work, he was going to have to break into Freddy Fazbear's.

Uncle Mike slid out from under the car he was working on. "Hey, kiddo," he said, smiling up at his nephew. "Ready to do some apprentice work for me today?"

"Sure," Colton said. He liked Uncle Mike's repair shop, its smell of grease and rubber, the tools lying around, the endless parade of cars to work on. He liked his bearded, paunchy uncle, too. If Colton continued to do well in his technical classes at school and apprenticed for Uncle Mike a couple of afternoons a week, Mike had promised Colton that he could have a job in the shop as soon as he graduated high school.

Mike wiped his hands on a grease-stained rag and nodded in the direction of a blue SUV. "Rear passenger tire on that one needs changing. I already got out the new tire and the tools you need. You know what you're doing, right?"

"Sure." Colton liked that Uncle Mike gave him credit for knowing some things. Colton had changed a lot of tires, mostly in Mike's shop but once on the side of the interstate when his mom's car had a blowout. His mom had made a big deal out of that, telling everybody she knew how he saved the day.

Colton worked efficiently at changing the tire. He felt most satisfied when he was working with his hands. Writing papers for school made him stressed out and frustrated, both when he had to write the paper and when he got the graded paper back with a C on it . . . if he was lucky. But he knew he was an A-plus student when it came to fixing things.

"Looks good, man," Uncle Mike said, surveying Colton's work. "Once I put in a new timing belt on this one over here, it needs an oil change. Think you're up for that?"

Colton smiled and nodded. He was good at oil changes, too.

"You want to watch me change the timing belt so you'll know how to do it?"

"Sure." Colton followed his uncle to the car. Once he had watched and learned, he got up his courage to ask Mike the question he had been waiting to ask him since he came to the shop. "Hey, Uncle Mike, I was wondering . . . could I borrow a few tools to use over the weekend? I've got a project I'm working on at home."

Mike grinned. "You know me and tools, kid. I've got extras of everything. When it comes to tools, I'm like some women are with shoes. Can't get enough of them."

Colton grinned back. "Yeah, but you don't ask to borrow somebody's shoes. That would be weird."

"True." Uncle Mike nodded in the direction of a large tool chest sitting against the wall. "You're welcome to borrow anything in there. Keep them for longer than the weekend if you need to. I know you'll take good care of them."

"Thanks, Uncle Mike." Colton felt a little guilty for not being honest about how he was going to use the tools, but not so guilty that he wasn't going to take what he needed.

After Colton finished the oil change and drank the soda that Uncle Mike brought him, he opened the chest to survey the tools. What tools would he need to get access to the inner workings of the Ticket

Pulverizer? There might be screws he would need to remove, so he grabbed a couple of different kinds of screwdrivers. A wrench seemed like it might be helpful and maybe a crowbar in case he needed to pry up the platform on the machine's floor. He needed to keep his tool kit pretty light, though. If he was going to be sneaking into the place, he couldn't be slowed down by carrying a lot of heavy equipment. He needed to be swift and stealthy, like a ninja.

Colton imagined himself dressed in black, moving smoothly and silently, breaking into Freddy's under the cover of night like a character in a movie. A little shiver of excitement ran through him.

Tools in hand, Colton left through the front office, where Uncle Mike was settling up with a customer.

"Thanks for letting me use your stuff, Uncle Mike."

"No problem," Uncle Mike said. He slipped Colton a ten-dollar bill from the cash register. Colton's apprenticeship wasn't a paid position, but it wasn't rare for Mike to hand him a little bit of cash. "This is for doing a good job lending me a hand today. And hey, if you need any help with that project, just let me know."

Colton smiled at the thought of asking Uncle Mike to help him break into Freddy Fazbear's to fix the Ticket Pulverizer. "Thanks, but I think I'd better handle this one on my own."

Colton had decided that Saturday night, the next time his mom worked an eight-to-eight shift, would be perfect for the Heist, as he had come to call it. But now it was Saturday afternoon, and he had just hit a major stumbling block.

Colton had gotten the right tools from Uncle Mike, and after lots of sketching and planning, he was pretty sure he knew what was needed to rerig the Ticket Pulverizer. But there was one obstacle he hadn't thought through.

He didn't know how to sneak into the building.

Sure, he had pictured himself in a black shirt and black pants and stocking cap, creeping around like a cat on the prowl. He had even pictured himself dodging lasers from the security system like he had seen in a movie once. But he didn't know how to get past the locked doors of Freddy Fazbear's. If he tried to pick the lock, surely an alarm would sound. If he tried to break the glass, an alarm would also sound and he could get busted for vandalism. Colton wanted to get into Freddy's to right a wrong, not to cause trouble. And he certainly didn't want to do anything to land himself in the juvenile detention center.

Colton was playing *Hammer of Odin* and trying to

relax so he could think clearly. His character was low on strength and weapons at the moment, so when a potential enemy became visible, Colton moved his character into a cave so he could hide from danger.

That's when a light switch turned on in Colton's brain.

He wouldn't try to break into Freddy's after it closed. He would hang out at Freddy's when it was open, like he did on a lot of Saturday nights. But when it got close to closing time, he wouldn't leave. He would hide. He would stay hidden until the employees had cleaned up the place and shut it down, and then he would come out and repair the Ticket Pulverizer.

By dinnertime, Colton was filled with nervous excitement. He sat across from his mom at the table, not making eye contact with her and toying with his food. The fluttering in his stomach seemed to be coming from something much stronger than butterflies.

"You're not eating much," Mom noted, looking over his plate. "Spaghetti and meatballs is usually your favorite. I even made extra thinking you'd at least go back for seconds and maybe thirds."

"Yeah, I know," Colton said, rolling a meatball across his plate with a fork. "The spaghetti's great. I just don't have much of an appetite."

His mom knitted her brow in concern. "Well,

that's certainly not like you. You're not coming down with something, are you? There's a nasty stomach bug going around. People have been coming into the ER with it all week. It's easy to get dehydrated when you can't keep anything down."

"I don't know," Colton said. "I guess I do feel a little tired." Colton wasn't tired at all, but it struck him that being "sick" might be a useful alibi. He yawned and stretched in what he hoped was a convincing display of fatigue.

"Hm," his mom said. "Well, if you don't feel any better, maybe you shouldn't go to Freddy's tonight. Being in a closed space with all those germy little kids certainly won't do your immune system—or everyone else's—any favors."

"True," Colton said, shuddering a little at the thought of all those little kids' germy paws, touching every surface they could reach, spreading disease like rats during the Black Plague. "If I don't feel better later, I'll stay home," he said, even though in his mind, he was already at Freddy's dismantling the Ticket Pulverizer.

"Good," Mom said, twirling spaghetti on her fork. "And if there's any kind of emergency, like if you were to get too sick to stay alone, call me at the third-floor nurses' station."

"I will, Mom. Thanks."

★ ★ ★

Once his mom left for work, Colton changed into black cargo pants, which were perfect since they were dark-colored but would also hold all his tools. The only problem was the tools were so heavy, once they were in his pockets, his pants immediately fell down. This, he decided, was probably not the best way to avoid calling attention to himself. He grabbed a belt from his closet and secured it tightly around his waist. He tucked his phone into his back right pocket and put the ten-dollar bill Uncle Mike had slipped him for helping in one of his many other pockets.

He felt afraid but also excited, like when he was about to go on a roller coaster.

One thought that especially gave him pleasure was the idea of getting tons and tons of tickets while Aidan and his annoying little friends got none. Aidan's disappointment would only add to Colton's joy. Why did the kid have to be so happy all the time? Even when Aidan was a baby, he had been all smiles. Babies were supposed to cry. Crying was normal.

It would be great to see his stupid cousin shed some tears for once, just like it would be great for Colton to come out a winner for once in his life.

He locked the door behind him and started the walk to Freddy's.

Freddy's was the usual riot of lights, sounds, and scurrying squeakers. It was two hours until closing time. *Just act casual*, Colton told himself. The best plan, he decided, was to lie low, play games, and try not to interact with the Freddy's employees. The more he could blend in, the better. He played the ball drop and the coin pusher a few times, rolled up the tickets he won into tight spools, and stuffed them in his cargo pants. As the clock crawled nearer to closing, he camped in the Skee-Ball section. For some reason—perhaps because wooden balls in the hands of toddlers were a safety hazard—the little kids tended to be kept away from the Skee-Ball area. Instead, this section was mostly occupied by dads killing time, who, Colton was sure, wouldn't notice him. Playing a few rounds of Skee-Ball seemed like a good way to win a few more tickets while keeping a low profile.

Before too long, a recorded Freddy Fazbear voice boomed over the intercom: "Sorry to spoil your fun, friends, but Freddy's will be closing in fifteen minutes. Come back tomorrow and play all day!"

Colton took a deep breath and tried to steady his nerves. It was time to swing into action. He was going to have to find a place to hide. He walked as casually as he could manage around the perimeter of the restaurant, looking for a room he could slip into unnoticed. The restrooms were out of the question, as someone would surely come in to clean them after closing time. And he certainly wasn't going to open the door marked OFFICE. Exploring further, he found another door, decorated with a poster of Freddy Fazbear and his weird-looking animal pals but otherwise unlabeled. He glanced around to make sure no one was looking, then tried the doorknob.

It turned.

As quietly and smoothly as he could, he opened the door and slipped behind it. *Ninja*, he thought to himself.

Colton found himself in a small storage room illuminated by a single, low-wattage light bulb. There was a rack of mops and brooms. Large yellow plastic buckets on wheels were lined up against the nearest wall. In front of the back wall was a tall gray metal cabinet with double doors. Could he hide inside the cabinet? Colton opened one of the doors. The cabinet was lined with shelves stocked with cleaning supplies and rolls of paper towels and toilet paper. There was no room to hide.

But then Colton noticed that the cabinet was not resting against the wall but was instead a few inches away from it. If he stood straight and held his breath, would it be possible for him to hide behind the cabinet?

It was worth a shot.

Colton took a deep breath, sucked in his stomach, and stood with his back flat to the wall. Inching sideways, he squeezed himself into the narrow space behind the cabinet. He had to turn his feet slightly sideways to make them fit. His grandmother was always telling him to stand up straight. Right now he was standing straighter than he had ever stood, his spine pressed against the wall. The back of the cabinet was touching his chest, and if he hadn't sucked in his stomach, it would be touching him there, too.

Colton had never really been in a tight space before, so he had never really understood claustrophobia. He understood it now. Even though he knew rationally that he had plenty of access to oxygen, he still had the sensation of not being able to breathe. The space was too tight, too cramped. He remembered reading a story about a man who was trapped in a cave and slowly went mad. Even after only being in this tiny space for a couple of minutes, he understood how quickly his sanity could slip away if he had no means of escaping.

But he was in control. He could leave his hiding place any time he wanted to. He was just choosing to stay there until closing time because it was the only way for his plan to work. He could do this.

And he had to admit to himself that it was an excellent hiding place. He surveyed all the dust bunnies he was sharing the space with and stifled a sneeze. Even if they were sneeze inducing, the dust bunnies were evidence that no one had moved this cabinet or even swept behind it in a long, long time.

If he could stay still and sneeze-less, he was going to be fine.

Colton could hear the voices of Freddy's employees outside the storage room, then the noise of a vacuum cleaner. He let his mind drift to images of himself jumping up and down in the repaired Ticket Pulverizer, literally buried in tickets, claiming his richly deserved prize. Daydreaming helped pass the time, helped distract from the physical discomfort of being pressed against a wall.

Colton heard the door to the supply room being pushed open, then footsteps.

"I don't know why I've always got to be the one to clean the toilets," an irritated-sounding female voice muttered. "Brittany the princess thinks she's too good to clean the bathrooms."

The footsteps approached the cabinet. Colton's heart pounded like a jackhammer.

Colton both heard and felt the Freddy's employee open the cabinet doors. If the back wall of the cabinet hadn't been separating them, she would be close enough to touch him.

Colton held his breath. *Don't let her hear you breathe*, he told himself.

"Okay, so spray cleaner and lots of toilet paper," the worker said. "Because goodness knows, Her Royal Highness Brittany couldn't lower herself to change a roll of toilet paper."

Colton heard the cabinet doors shut and the worker's footsteps walking away from him. The storage room was empty again.

Colton exhaled.

He let his mind drift—it could have been for a couple of minutes or an hour—he was losing track of time. But then he heard the flip of a switch, and the room was plunged into darkness.

A flashlight. Why had he not brought a flashlight? What if the entire restaurant was pitch-black? How could he work on the Ticket Pulverizer then?

Stupid, he chided himself. *How could you be so stupid?*

Soon the noises of human movement outside the storage room faded, and Freddy's fell silent. Colton slowly slid from behind the storage cabinet. His back hurt, and his shoulders were stiff. It was a relief to stretch.

The supply room was so dark he had to use the light from his phone to find his way to the door. He hoped that when he opened it, he wouldn't be greeted by more darkness.

The fluorescent lights in the game area had been turned off, but security lights on the ceiling, along with the colorful lights from the various token-sucking games, still illuminated the arcade. The glow of the games in the dim room had an effect that was somewhat eerie, but at least Colton could see. He could do what he came here to do.

Colton made his way to the Ticket Pulverizer. He unloaded his tools from his pockets and laid them out on the floor. He couldn't help but smile to himself. His plan had worked. He was in. He felt like an action hero.

He had thought a lot about the mechanics of the Ticket Pulverizer and why it worked unfairly well for the annoying little brats. He figured the platform was too loose, too easy for them to push down. If he could tighten it up, make it more resistant, then the little brats couldn't make it budge, and there would be more tickets for the older, bigger, and more deserving.

Colton fed four tokens into the Ticket Pulverizer to make the door open. Once he was inside, it didn't take him long to figure out where to tighten the platform. A few turns of the screwdriver on each corner, and the platform was much more rigid and required a lot more weight to move it.

He was sorely tempted to feed in some more tokens and jump for tickets right then and there. But the jumping was noisy, and he didn't want to do anything that might call attention to himself. He gave the platform a small, experimental push and whispered "Mission accomplished" before exiting the booth.

But as he stood in the middle of the empty arcade, the reality of his situation dawned on him. His mission wasn't totally accomplished. He still needed to get out of Freddy's. He had spent so much time planning out how to get into Freddy's and work on the Pulverizer that he had forgotten to plan how to get out.

He had no exit strategy.

Colton looked around at the doors marked EXIT. He was sure each of them was equipped with a security alarm. He scanned the room frantically. Maybe there was a back door he could use. Maybe in the kitchen. He walked through a dim hallway and pushed open the door to the kitchen. It was pitch-black, so he held up his phone to light his way past the huge ovens and cooktops. Around the corner, he saw a door and felt a rush of relief, but when he looked up, he saw the security alarm.

Colton's breath was short and ragged. He couldn't just stay here until Freddy's opened up again at eleven o'clock the next morning and say, "Oops, guys, I guess I got locked in." Plus, if his mom got home from work in the morning and he wasn't there, she would panic.

Think, Colton told himself. *There has to be a way out.*

Colton thought back over all his visits to Freddy's. He had been coming to Freddy's since he was a loathsome little squeaker himself, so he knew the place well. He thought about the layout of the building. Finally, an image popped into his head. The restroom. Wasn't there a window in the men's restroom?

The restroom was as dark as the kitchen. Colton held up his phone for enough light to make out the shapes of the sinks and stalls and—*yes!*—the window. It was a small window, too high up to access easily, but he could get to it if he stood on one of the chairs from the dining area. He'd have to leave the chair behind in the bathroom, which wasn't ideal, but it was better than spending the whole night at Freddy's.

He went back to the dining area, retrieved a chair, and carried it to the restroom. He set it under the window and climbed onto it. He was worried that the window wouldn't open, but it pushed up easily, and no alarm sounded. Grunting with effort, he pulled himself through the opening and plummeted to the ground, landing on his hands and knees with an "Oof!" Some of Uncle Mike's tools fell from his pockets.

He was a little shaken, but he was okay. Now all he had to do was gather up the tools and walk home like everything was normal. When his mom got home from her Saturday-night shift, she'd find him in bed like nothing had happened.

And tomorrow afternoon he'd go back to Freddy's where he'd be the king of the Ticket Pulverizer.

★ ★ ★

Colton had only five dollars to take with him to Freddy's, but he figured that would be enough. Five dollars equaled five turns inside the Ticket Pulverizer, and by that time, he'd be rolling in tickets.

Once he got there, he didn't bother with the ball drop or the coin pusher. He made a beeline to the Ticket Pulverizer just in time to see a group of three little kids go inside, shrieking and giggling. He smiled to himself. *This should be entertaining. Stupid squeakers don't suspect a thing.*

He watched the little kids gleefully jump up and down. Tickets poured down like water flowing from a faucet. How could that be? After the way he'd fixed it, their weight shouldn't have been enough to trigger such an outpouring of tickets. Colton seethed with rage.

Maybe, though, he'd at least fixed things so he would get a lot of tickets, too. Maybe he had just turned the Pulverizer into a machine that heaped tickets on anyone who went inside. As long as he got his fair share, he guessed that was okay.

The little kids came out, holding fat ribbons of tickets in their equally fat little fists. Colton elbowed his way past them. It was his turn.

He put four tokens into the slot and stepped into the Ticket Pulverizer. His heart was beating fast in anticipation. He knew this was it; this time he was going to get what he deserved.

The lights in the sign reading JUMP FOR TICKETS started flashing. Colton jumped. In his mind, he was a jackrabbit, a kangaroo, any animal he could think of with strong legs and big feet and mighty jumping power. He jumped and jumped, but only a trickle of tickets fell. How could that be after all the planning, all the hard work, that went into his heist? It didn't make sense. The madder he got, the harder he jumped.

Only a few tickets drifted listlessly to the floor.

When time was up, he was so furious that he stomped out of the machine and left the tickets where they were. There weren't enough of them to do him any good anyway.

On the walk home, his anger turned into dejection. Why did life have to be so unfair? Why did some people have so much while people like Colton and his mom had so little? It was just luck, wasn't it? Some people had good luck, and some people had bad luck. It was pretty obvious what kind of luck he had. But couldn't luck change? Surely there had to be some way to game the system.

Back at the apartment, Colton's mom was humming to herself while she chopped onions. Tears were in her eyes from the smell, but she had the day off and seemed to be in a good mood. Colton sank into a kitchen chair.

"Hey," his mom said. "I'm making sloppy joes. Have you ever thought about what a weird name that is for a sandwich? Like, was there actually a guy named Joe who looked really messy all the time? And then one day somebody said, 'Hey, Joe, we're naming a sandwich after you,' and he was all like, 'Wow, that's great!' But then it turned out they were calling them sloppy joes. And he was like, 'Wait, you're calling them what?'"

Colton usually laughed at his mom's weird flights of fancy, but today he couldn't find the energy to respond.

"What's the matter, Colt? Not even a smile?" His mom tapped him with her spatula. "You usually think my tangents are funny."

Cory shrugged. "Just not in a smiling mood, I guess."

His mom sat down at the table across from him. "Any particular reason you want to talk about?"

"Not really. Just tired of seeing other people get what I deserve. People who don't deserve it, like little kids. They've not been around long enough to deserve anything. They've not paid their dues yet. They might as well still be in diapers." The more he thought about it, the angrier he felt.

"Rough time at Freddy's today, huh?" his mom asked.

"Yeah, the stupid Ticket Pulverizer again," he said. He'd complained about it enough that his mom understood what he was talking about.

"No luck with it?"

Colton shook his head. "I'm never going to get enough tickets to get what I want."

"Well, I've been thinking about it, and you know, there are other ways of getting what you want," Mom said, pulling her hair back with the rubber band she kept around her wrist.

Colton didn't think he liked his mom's tone. It was the same tone she used when she was about to nag him to do his homework or chores. "What do you mean?"

"Well," his mom said, "I had a part-time job when I was your age. I worked at the Swirly Cone after school and on weekends, making cones and shakes and sundaes. It didn't pay much, but the money adds up when you don't have any other expenses."

Colton couldn't help but feel offended. "Are you telling me I have to get a job? I already help Uncle Mike out two days a week."

"I'm not telling you that you *have* to. I'm just saying it's an option. If you worked, say, ten to fifteen hours a week, you could save up money to buy those luxury items I can't afford. If you keep throwing money at the Ticket Pulverizer, you'll probably have spent more money trying to win tickets than that video game console costs anyway."

Colton stood up from his chair. He was outraged. "I can't believe you're trying to make me get a job.

I'm just a kid! Haven't you ever heard of child labor laws?"

His mom rolled her eyes. "You are legally old enough to have a part-time job. Kids younger than you earn money mowing lawns or doing odd jobs for people. There's no reason you couldn't do something like that. Or you could see if Mike would give you a few hours a week at minimum wage. It feels good to earn your own money, Colton. It's just something to think about."

"What's the point of having a cool video game console if you don't have time to play it because you're working all the time?" Colton felt his voice getting louder. "If Dad was still here, we wouldn't have to worry about money."

For a moment, his mom looked hurt, almost as if he had struck her, but then her expression shifted to irritation. "No, we wouldn't. But he isn't here, so we have to do the best we can." She got up from the table and went back to the stove. "Dinner will be ready in twenty minutes. Between now and then, why don't you see if you can get over your bad mood?"

Colton didn't get over his bad mood. He lay in his bed playing the same scene over and over in his head: those repulsive little kids laughing and cheering as an avalanche of tickets fell on them. He didn't understand why his attempt to fix the Ticket Pulverizer had failed. There had to be another way to do it.

He got out of bed, went to his desk, and started making sketches of the machine. Screwing the platform in tighter hadn't been enough. He should have known it wasn't going to be that easy. To solve this problem, he was going to have to dig deeper.

Colton had become obsessed with the Ticket Pulverizer. He looked up similar kinds of machines online, trying to get a better understanding of their mechanics.

Today, in shop class, he sat furiously sketching and making notes, as he had done in class every day for the past week.

Mr. Harrison, the fatherly, balding shop teacher, leaned over his shoulder. "Colton, you've been drawing and making notes for ages. What is it you're designing?"

Colton knew he couldn't tell Mr. Harrison what he was really doing. He knew no adults would understand his obsession. Colton wasn't even sure he understood it himself, but he knew he couldn't stop until he finally experienced justice from the Ticket Pulverizer.

"It's more of a plan for fixing something," Colton said, still furiously sketching.

Mr. Harrison raised an eyebrow. "I can appreciate that, but you know that if you don't actually *make* something, I can't give you a grade, right?"

"Right," Colton said, not looking up from his notebook. He was relieved when Mr. Harrison walked away to talk to other students. He didn't care if he got a grade or not. Right now, anything that didn't pertain to the Ticket Pulverizer felt like an unneeded interruption.

That night, Colton brought his notebook with him to the dinner table. He sketched and wrote notes between bites of meat loaf and mashed potatoes and peas, which, due to his distraction, he didn't even really taste.

"I have Sunday off this weekend for the first time in ages," his mom said. "I thought we might do something fun together. Maybe pack a picnic and drive up to the mountains. Go on a little hike. We could stop on the way home for ice cream at that place you like."

"Mm-hm," Colton said absently. He was aware that his mom was talking, but he hadn't actually processed any of her words.

"Colton," Mom said, "you're a million miles away, and you have been for over a week now. What is it that you're working on day and night?" She gestured at his notebook.

"It's just a project for school," Colton mumbled, not looking up.

"Well, I hope it is," Mom said, pushing away her plate of half-eaten food, "because I ran into your English teacher yesterday, and she says she's worried about you. She says you've not been turning in your assignments, and your grade has slipped to a low D. 'And D means danger,' according to her. Is there a reason you're falling behind in your work?"

Colton finally looked up. If he didn't get his mom off his back, he wasn't going to be able to make his plan work. "I'll talk to her tomorrow about what I need to do to catch up in class."

His mom nodded. "Okay. I know you don't like to talk about emotional stuff, but is there anything you need to say to me? Anything that's bothering you?" She looked sad, as if she might cry, which Colton desperately hoped she wouldn't. "I know since I work a lot of nights, it may feel like I'm not here when you need me, and I'm sorry for that. But where it counts, I'm always here for you, Colton." She covered his hand with her own. "Just don't shut me out, okay?"

"Okay, Mom. Sheesh." Colton drew his hand away. He was more than ready for this conversation to end.

"So . . . there's nothing you want to talk about?"

"Nope." He went back to his sketching.

Mom sighed and got up from her chair. "Okay.

Guess I'd better get ready for work. Will you load the dishwasher for me?"

"Uh-huh," Colton said, forgetting the promise as soon as he made it.

Once his mom was gone, he left for Freddy's. He had only two bucks in his pocket, which wouldn't go very far in the arcade. But he wasn't there to play games. He was there to observe the Ticket Pulverizer.

Colton stood a few steps away from the machine that consumed his every waking hour. He looked at it as an enemy to be defeated. Like in one of those Greek myths he had read in middle school, he was the hero, and it was the monster. And the clown—the horrible, gape-jawed clown—was like a dragon standing guard that he had to defeat before his big battle with the boss monster. He watched as group after group of loathsome little kids trooped into the machine and jumped up and down and stamped their tiny feet while the tickets poured out, not like a faucet but like a waterfall.

It was so unfair, it sickened him.

A little girl with a blond ponytail, who was maybe eight or nine years old, came marching up to him. "Hey, why do you keep staring at the people inside the Ticket Pulverizer?" she said. She pronounced the word *pulverizer* carefully, like she was sounding it out.

Colton was incensed. How dare this little brat approach him and talk to him in such a judgmental way? Where were her parents? "I'm not watching the people. I'm watching the machine," he said in a cold, measured tone.

"Well, my friend over there says you're creepy," the little girl said.

Colton looked over at a dark-haired girl who was standing by the Ticket Pulverizer and staring at them as they talked. Her eyes were big and unblinking, and her gaze was penetrating. "Tell your friend the feeling is mutual."

The little girl crinkled her nose. "I don't even know what that means."

"If you don't know what it means," Colton said, deepening his voice in hopes of sounding adult and intimidating, "then maybe that means you're not old enough to be starting conversations with somebody older than you." He made a shooing gesture, as if she were a pesky gnat. "Go. Away."

"I'm happy to go away from you," the little girl said, turning her back on him and flouncing back to her friend.

"Good, then go," Colton muttered.

The little girl was annoying, but she had told him something he needed to know. By scoping out the Ticket Pulverizer, he was calling unwanted attention to himself. If he was going to pull this off, he had to go unnoticed. He couldn't have horrible little girls noticing him and thinking he was creepy. And he certainly couldn't do anything to attract the attention of the Freddy's staff. He needed to be invisible— silent and stealthy. *Like a ninja*, he reminded himself.

Colton walked away from the Ticket Pulverizer and toward the exit. He had seen what he needed to see.

By Friday night, Colton's plan was complete. This time he wouldn't do his work at night. He would work in daylight so he could see what he was doing. He would set his alarm for 6:00 a.m. and would sneak into Freddy's before it opened. He figured if he had successfully used the restroom window to sneak out, he could also use it to sneak in.

Before he went to bed, he laid out his necessities: a dark shirt, his cargo pants, his phone, and the tools he would stuff in the pockets. And this time, even though it was day, he was taking a flashlight. If he was going to go deep inside the dark innards of the Ticket Pulverizer, he needed to be able to see what he was doing.

Colton lay in bed, wide-awake, running through the Heist over and over in his mind. The one thing that was worrying him was the bathroom window. He had used a chair for the boost he needed to get out of it, but how was he going to get into it? He couldn't exactly take a step ladder with him and prop it against the building without practically announcing, "*Don't mind me, folks. I'm just doing some breaking and entering here.*" He would just have to improvise. He'd get through the window somehow.

Finally, excitement gave way to exhaustion, and Colton fell asleep. In his dreams, he jumped up and down on the Pulverizer's platform, and tickets cascaded over him until they were waist-high, then shoulder-high in them. He was literally swimming in tickets. People watching him cheered. He had never felt such joy.

When the alarm went off, his eyes flew open. This was it. Today was the day he was going to make it work. He took off his pajamas and put on the dark shirt and cargo pants. He loaded the tools in his pockets and tightened his belt as an added precaution. He stopped in the kitchen and wolfed down a banana and chugged a glass of orange juice. He was ready.

The streets were largely deserted at 6:30 a.m., which was another reason Colton congratulated himself on the brilliance of his plan. No witnesses.

Once he reached the Freddy's building, he walked around the side and found the bathroom window. If he stood on tiptoe, he could just reach the windowsill with his fingertips. He groaned in disappointment. There was no way he had the upper body strength to pull himself up. He was going to have to find something to climb on. He walked farther around the building. Next to the back door was a lidded garbage can on wheels. *Perfect*, Colton thought.

The handle of the garbage can was sticky with something Colton didn't want to think about, but he hung on to it anyway and rolled the can to the side of the building. The wheels made a little more noise than he would have liked, but there didn't seem to be anyone around to hear it. He positioned the garbage can right under the window and awkwardly climbed on top of it. The can's plastic lid warped under his weight, and the wheels made him feel unsteady. But he pushed up the window, grabbed the sill, and started dragging himself through, headfirst.

Soon he was awkwardly hanging with his hands in the sink and his feet still sticking out the window. Not sure what else to do, he pushed his feet off the windowsill and flipped forward, hitting the floor hard on his backside. It didn't tickle, and the wind was knocked out of him, but he wasn't injured.

And most important, he was *in*.

He pulled himself clumsily to his feet and waited a minute for his breathing to return to normal. How was it that in the movies, people could jump from a great height, land hard, and then hop right up and keep on running?

When Colton swung open the bathroom door,

the clown animatronic was standing in the hallway, almost as if it had been waiting for him. Colton jumped backward, his heart beating fast. "Yeesh!" he said, looking at the thing's horrible gape-mouthed grin. "Shouldn't somebody put you away at night?" He squeezed past the clown, fearful that it might grab him, but it just stood there like the inanimate object it was.

Still, when Colton walked down the hallway, it was hard not to look back to see if the clown was following him.

Colton didn't think he'd ever get used to this silent version of Freddy's. No screaming rug rats, no bleeping games, no prerecorded songs and chatter from Freddy's animatronic band. It was quieter than a library.

Then Colton heard a faint jingling.

Or at least he thought he did. It was the soft, tinkly noise that the bells on the birthday clown's costume would make. Was the clown following him?

Colton had to laugh at himself. Of course the clown wasn't following him. It was a machine, a thing. It was no more capable of stalking somebody than a vacuum cleaner.

He heard the jingling again. Closer this time.

He ducked behind BB's Ball Drop and listened for the bells. He heard nothing.

When he stepped out from behind the machine,

he saw the clown. It was at the end of the row of games with its back turned to him. Colton hurried as quietly as he could in the opposite direction.

Jingle, jingle.

The clown was on the move again. Colton squatted down beside DeeDee's Fishing Game. His heart was pounding in his chest. He held his breath as the clown shambled past him, bells tinkling.

It's not looking for you, Colton told himself. *Stop acting like a stupid squeaker. You can't get all spooked by a dumb fake clown and lose the opportunity that's right here for the taking. You know why you came here.*

He made his way to the Ticket Pulverizer. When he got there, the clown was standing in front of the machine as if it were guarding it. But when Colton waved his hand in front of the clown's eyes, it didn't react at all. One eye looked ahead and one looked down and off to the right, like always. And of course they weren't really *looking* anyway, Colton told himself. The clown's eyes were as unseeing as the button eyes on Colton's childhood teddy bear. He couldn't let the creepy clown distract him from his mission. Colton stared at the Ticket Pulverizer. Its lights flashed and glowed. It felt like an enemy issuing a challenge. But soon, Colton thought, he would tame the Ticket Pulverizer, and it would be a faithful friend, giving him the rewards he so richly deserved.

He walked around the machine, surveying its base. On one side, he spotted what looked like the larger version of a battery compartment cover on a TV remote control. If he could get that cover open, he might be able to squeeze into the base of the machine to tinker with its workings.

Colton dug through his pockets to find the tools he needed. He set out his phone, a screwdriver, and a flashlight.

Colton felt a hand on his shoulder, but it wasn't a normal human hand. He looked down to see a large three-fingered white glove connected to telltale yellow coils.

"Get off me!" he yelled. He slapped the hand away, then whirled around and shoved the clown as hard as he could in its midsection. It hurtled backward, crashed into an arcade cabinet, and fell onto its side.

Colton was amazed how lightweight the clown was and how far he had been able to push it. Seeing it lying there on the floor, it looked like a broken toy, certainly not like anything to be scared of. He got down on his knees and pulled on the cover. It flipped open easily. Clearly it was a hatch that allowed access to the Pulverizer's innards. The opening was small, no bigger than the bathroom window Colton had used to break into Freddy's.

Colton dropped his screwdriver inside the door,

and then, turning on his flashlight, he crawled into the machine.

The space inside was cramped. There was no room to sit up. He could only lie down with his legs bent sideways in an uncomfortable position, with the bottom of the machine's platform touching the length of his body. Shining his flashlight around, he was relieved to see that the mechanical parts looked how he expected them to look. It was just going to be hard for him to do the work he needed to do from an awkward reclining position.

Colton squinted at the inner workings of the Ticket Pulverizer. As he started to loosen a screw, he felt something tightly grip his ankles. He shined his flashlight to see a pair of white-gloved hands, one grasping each ankle. The yellow coil arms were stretched out long, but they contracted as they pulled his body toward the opening where he had entered the compartment.

How could the clown weigh so little and yet be so strong? It had pulled his legs straight and was dragging him out of the machine. Once Colton's legs were outside, he wrenched his right one free and threw a bunch of wild, hard kicks that he felt connect with the clown's body. After one particularly forceful kick, the clown loosened its grip on his other leg, and Colton scrambled to get his full body back into the base of the Pulverizer. Once he was inside, he closed the hatch he had entered through behind him. The clown's hands were large, awkward things, and he hoped it would lack the motor skills needed to pull the hatch back open. Besides, from the strength of his kicks, maybe he'd put the clown out of commission anyway.

Now it was time for Colton to steady his hands and his nerves and do what he came here to do.

Even with the flashlight, it took a few minutes for his eyes to adjust to the darkness. It was like being in a small, tight alcove in a cave. Memories of the claustrophobic closet in the back room of Freddy's momentarily rushed back to him, but when he shined his flashlight on the machinery, he smiled. He knew what he needed to do. It was going to be challenging because he needed both hands to do his work, but there was no place to set the flashlight, which he needed so he could see.

Finally, he awkwardly secured the flashlight under his left armpit and angled the beam to hit the area he needed to work on.

All his reading, planning, and obsessing had paid off. Even though he was working under less-than-ideal conditions, the process of fixing the Pulverizer couldn't have gone more smoothly. At some point he'd realized the trick: Flip these switches to tie the ticket release to the size of the bounces. Loosen these screws to give the platform even more bounce. The little kids would get more tickets, sure, but big kids like Colton would be flush with them.

Colton smiled at his achievement. *People didn't give him the credit he deserved*, he thought. His teachers didn't comprehend who they were dealing with. They thought he was just some regular high school freshman, a C student. Average, no different from a thousand other kids. His mom, even though she loved him, didn't give him enough credit either. Only Colton could see the truth about himself. He was brilliant, a mechanical genius.

With his newly realized self-confidence, his luck was sure to change. The thousands of tickets he was going to win from the Ticket Pulverizer were only the beginning.

Colton smiled at his handiwork one last time, then reached over his head to push the small door open so he could climb out and make his exit.

The door wouldn't budge.

There has to be some kind of mistake, Colton thought. He pushed the door again, harder this time. It still refused to move. It was like it was locked from the outside. But how was that possible? No one was in Freddy's, and even if they were, why would they suspect someone was inside the Ticket Pulverizer?

He shoved it again. It held fast.

Colton shined his flashlight around the tiny space,

trying to see if there might be another way to get out, a panel that could be removed or something. There was nothing.

Colton's flashlight found a small round hole about the size of the head of a bolt. It was just big enough to peek through. Colton closed one eye and looked through the tiny opening with the other. All he could see were big green shoes. Clown shoes. It was standing guard there, waiting. If it couldn't get him out of the machine itself, it would wait until he found a way to get out on his own. He thought of an expression his uncle used sometimes: *between a rock and a hard place*. He had never really understood the meaning of that saying until now.

He felt himself starting to shake. His heart thudded in his chest so loud that he could hear it. Somehow he felt sweaty and cold at the same time. The space seemed to shrink around him until it was squeezing him from all sides. He lay with his knees hugged to his chest, trying to make himself smaller so the space would seem larger.

It'll be okay, he told himself. In two or three hours, Freddy's would open, and somebody could rescue him. But how could he stand to stay in this tiny place in this uncomfortable position for two or three hours? Was there even enough air to keep him alive that long? Already the air he was breathing felt scarce and stale. And assuming someone did rescue him, how would he explain himself? *I was playing Jump for Tickets last night, and I guess I jumped so hard I fell in. Oops.*

He was going to have to come up with a more credible story.

Colton looked down at his flashlight. He had no idea how much life the batteries still had in them. It was probably best to try to conserve them. He switched off the flashlight and was plunged into total darkness. He remembered a story he'd read in school about a man trapped in the deep blackness of a coal mine, waiting to die. He felt like that man.

He tried to let his mind wander. He made lists of things: favorite video games, favorite movies, favorite foods. But the last one was a bad idea because it made him realize how hungry he was. He usually ate a full breakfast, but today he'd had nothing but that banana. He was thirsty, too. It had never occurred to him to bring water because he hadn't thought that he might be trapped like this.

Colton's stomach lurched, not with hunger but with nausea. The acid from the orange juice he had drunk earlier seemed to be upsetting his stomach. But he knew it wasn't really the orange juice that was affecting him. It was fear. Fear was eating away at his insides and making him sick.

Don't throw up, don't throw up, Colton told himself. If he threw up in here, he would be trapped in this tiny space with the horrible smell of his own vomit. He sucked in great gulps of air, trying to quell his nausea. But then, he worried, what if he was being too greedy with the air? What if he was using the *limited* supply of oxygen in this tiny space too quickly?

Both of Colton's legs had fallen asleep, but there was no room to move them around to wake them up. He wiggled his toes and moved his feet at his ankles, all the time feeling like he was being pricked by hundreds of needles. His neck was starting to cramp, and he pivoted his head from side to side, trying to relieve the pain.

But the pain and sickness weren't the worst parts. The worst part was the question gnawing at the back of Colton's mind: *What if no one finds me? What if nobody hears me and I die from thirst or hunger? Will somebody find me when my body starts to rot? Or will all that's left of me be a dusty, forgotten skeleton, curled up in this compartment for years and years like a mummy in its tomb?*

But he also knew that curling up and dying inside the machine might not be the worst thing that could happen to him. From outside the machine, he heard jingling as the clown patrolled back and forth in front of the Ticket Pulverizer. He thought again of the mice who wanted to hang the bell on the cat so they would know when their killer was close. Colton shuddered. Maybe it was better not to know.

Clearly, sitting here in the dark like this was making him a little crazy. He turned on the flashlight for just a couple of seconds as a reality check. At least he knew he could still see. Good. But when he turned off the light and was surrounded by darkness again, he felt scared of the dark as though he was a little kid. It was like this terrible experience was making him move backward in time, becoming the child he had once been. The child that he hated, like he hated all children.

But wait. Colton remembered something. His phone. He had his phone. If all else failed, he could call his mom, confess to his crimes, and get rescued. She was probably already home from her shift and wondering where he was. He reached into his right back pocket. It was empty. He tried the left back one even though he knew he hadn't put it there. He patted down all his pockets frantically. And then a picture flashed in his mind: him setting out the phone and his tools on the floor beside the machine, opening the machine's door, and dropping the tools inside *but not the phone.*

Colton said some words his mother didn't allow him to say.

Then, as if on cue, he heard it. A faint ringing coming from just outside the machine. His ringtone. He was sure it was his mom, calling to see if he was okay.

Colton was not okay.

He pushed on the door with his full strength. It was like trying to move a solid brick wall. He pushed on the platform just above him. It was useless.

Colton peeked through the tiny hole in the Ticket Pulverizer's base. He saw his phone on the black-and-white tile floor, vibrating as it rang. And then a white-gloved, three-fingered hand reached down and picked it up. "No!" he screamed. "No! No! No!" He screamed till his throat was raw, knowing the whole time that it wouldn't make any difference.

Time passed. How much? An hour? Five minutes? Colton had no idea. In the dark, with nothing to do and nothing to see, time lost its meaning. Other things started to lose their meaning, too. Colton started to find it hard to form words in his mind. He knew the physical sensations he was feeling: thirst, hunger, pain from his body being cramped into an unnatural position, the uncomfortable pressure of a full bladder. But he couldn't find the words for any of these things. He could only feel them and whimper softly and wait.

He wasn't even sure anymore what he was waiting for.

Scared, unable to use language or feed himself, in very real danger of wetting his pants, Colton was regressing to the helplessness of an infant. If he continued to go backward physically and emotionally, the next logical step would be to disappear into nothingness, to become one with the darkness.

For a while, it seemed as if it had happened, that Colton had simply ceased to exist, but then he heard it. And if he could hear, it must mean that he existed. It was the music, the bleeping and blipping of the games, the annoying voices of the animatronic characters. Colton remembered where he was and what his predicament was.

But things were looking up. Noises meant people. If Freddy's was open for business, somebody was there to hear him.

He started out by yelling for help but quickly realized his throat was too dry and his voice too weak from disuse to make much noise. Instead, he banged on the platform with his fists. He hit the stupid thing over and over but with no results. His knuckles ached and would probably bruise. He figured no one was nearby and decided to conserve his energy. If he kept banging on the platform continuously, he would only exhaust himself. He would wait a little while until there were some customers, then try again.

Like a cat washing its paws, Colton licked his knuckles, trying to soothe his pain with the moisture of his saliva. But his tongue was too dry from thirst to be of much use.

At least now the terrible darkness was no longer

accompanied by silence. If he could hear noises, he knew he was alive.

From the sound of little footsteps and high-pitched yelling and giggling, it was clear that Freddy's had now opened for business. And when Freddy's was full of overstimulated rug rats, it was the noisiest place on earth.

It was amazing how much Colton could hear from his tiny prison. He could pick out the sounds of different video games. He recognized sound effects that accompanied BB's Ball Drop and the annoying jingly tune that played when someone put in a token to play DeeDee's Fishing Hole. He could hear the canned music of Freddy Fazbear's band as they launched into the birthday song. He could hear some obnoxious child whining, "But why isn't it *my* happy birthday?"

Normally, the sounds at Freddy's all jumbled together in a big, noisy soup. But Colton could hear everything individually, like hearing was his superpower. Maybe when you had been isolated from some of your senses, the ones you could still use became stronger.

Right now, for example, Colton was hearing Coils the Birthday Clown's prerecorded voice say, "Get ready for the Ticket Pulverizer Countdown!"

There was the sound of little kids screaming and cheering.

"Now who's ready to Jump! For! Tickets!" Coils said, its voice actor feigning excitement.

Colton knew what would happen next. Some Freddy's employee would open the door of the Ticket Pulverizer and let in all the overexcited birthday party kids.

This was great. If people were in the Pulverizer—even if they were stupid little kids—Colton could get them to notice him. They could tell an adult that they heard screaming under the platform, and he would be saved. Colton breathed a sigh of relief. This ordeal would be over soon.

He could feel them above him, jostling around and bumping into one another. The platform pressed down on him a little more from their weight. They were giggling and talking to one another in little kid gibberish.

Colton suddenly became aware of how urgent his situation was. If the platform was already pressing down on him more from the little kids just standing there, he had to get their attention before they started jumping. His repair to the machine would make the platform dip even lower into his crawl space.

Colton banged on the bottom of the platform. "Hey!" he yelled as loudly as he could with his dry, scratchy throat. "Hey! I'm down here! Help me! Help!"

He was going to have to try harder if he was going

to make himself heard over all the noises of the place, plus the noisiness of the kids themselves. He pounded on the bottom of the platform with his hammer. "Help!" he screamed. "I'm trapped in here! Help! Help!"

"Prepare for the Ticket Pulverizer Countdown! Now, when I finish counting, everybody jump up and down as hard as you can, all together," the clown's prerecorded voice said.

The children's screams of excitement drowned out Colton's screams for help.

"Here we go!" the clown announced. "Ten, nine, eight, seven, six, five, four, three, two . . . one! Now . . . Jump! For! Tickets!"

Overhead, Bella the birthday girl and her six friends jumped in unison, the sound like a stampede of wild buffalo. The platform dropped, they laughed and cheered, and the tickets fell like rain.

But then something wasn't right. Bella had jumped in the Ticket Pulverizer lots of times. This time felt different. The platform wasn't dropping as low as usual. The flow of tickets had slowed to a trickle. "It's slowing down!" she yelled to her friend Aidan.

"Jump harder!" Aidan yelled back.

Bella jumped higher and landed with more force. The platform dropped. Some tickets sprinkled down, but it was a light shower, not the flood of tickets Bella wanted for her birthday.

"Let's all hold hands and jump together!" Bella yelled.

"I don't want to hold hands!" Aidan yelled back.

"Come on, it's my birthday!" Bella said.

Aidan shrugged and relented, and the seven kids joined in a circle.

"One . . . two . . . three . . . jump!" Bella yelled. The kids leaped, then landed at the same time, forcing the platform down, then up, then down farther.

Jump. The platform dropped an inch.

Jump. And another inch.

Jump. And another. Bella and her friends laughed and let go of each other so they could grab the falling tickets.

After the next jump, though, the platform didn't go any lower. The kids jumped again, but it stayed put.

Bella looked out at her dad, who was outside the Ticket Pulverizer, cheering them on.

"It's not working!" she yelled.

"Jump harder, sweetie!" her dad called back.

Jump.

Jump.

Jump.

The kids all jumped with as much force as they possibly could. The platform lowered a tiny bit more, less than an inch, then wobbled a little, then stopped.

One lonely ticket fell from the machine's ceiling.

Outside the Ticket Pulverizer, Bella's dad nudged his wife. "That game's broken," he said. "The platform's not dropping like it should. I think I'm going to go get a manager." He was already looking around, trying to spot who was in charge.

"Good idea," Bella's mom said. Looking inside the Ticket Pulverizer, she could see that even though the children were still jumping away, they were getting increasingly frustrated. The platform was pretty much stationary.

In a few minutes, Bella's dad returned with a heavyset Freddy's employee whose name tag read TED. He gave the machine a once-over. "You're right," he said. "The thing's busted someway." He squatted, reached down under the machine, and switched it off.

The children looked shocked by the sudden absence of light and noise.

"I'm sorry, kids," Ted said, yelling over the general chaos of Freddy's. "The Ticket Pulverizer isn't working right. I need you guys to get out of the machine, but I'll tell you what. Since you didn't get to win much in there, if you all go up to the front counter, the cashier will give you twenty free tickets each."

The kids' moods got sunnier as they exited the machine and ran in the direction of the free tickets.

The clown animatronic was acting weird, too. It

was pointing at the base of the machine and grabbing at Ted's arm as if it didn't want him to go inside the Ticket Pulverizer. But of course it didn't *want* anything. It was just a stupid robot. A stupid robot that seemed to be malfunctioning. Ted shook his head. Was every cheap piece of equiment in this run-down place breaking all at the same time? Ted climbed into the Pulverizer and jumped on the platform a few times. It hardly moved, even with the force of all his ample weight, though he did think he heard a liquidy squishing sound that, of course, made no sense. He was going to have to call the repair guy.

When Ted exited the machine, the clown robot was standing in front of the door. Its face, which was usually wearing a comically huge grin, was now a mask of tragedy, with a downturned mouth and sad-looking eyes. Was a tear sliding down its cheek, or was Ted imagining things? Sometimes he thought he should find a more normal place to work.

One of the little kids from the Ticket Pulverizer must have noticed the clown's sad face, too, because he ran up to it and said, "Hey, Coils, remember me? I'm your buddy Aiden. Don't be sad, okay? It's bad to be sad. My cousin Colton's sad all the time. That's why I'm saving up my tickets to buy him a present."

The little boy threw his arms around the clown animatronic, and it hugged him back, holding him in its springy, coiled yellow arms.

Weird, Ted thought, walking past the scene on the way to his office.

The Ticket Pulverizer stood empty, or at least empty as far as anyone could see. Ted returned from his office with a sign that he hung on the machine's door: OUT OF ORDER.

PIZZA
KIT

"I can't believe you talked me into taking home ec," Payton said as she sat down with her best friend, Marley, at a long table in the classroom. "Who takes home ec these days?"

"Come on, it's an easy A," Marley said, taking a notebook out of her backpack. "I mean, look around. How hard could it be?"

Surveying the classroom, Payton had to admit that Marley might have a point. The room was lined with kitchen counters, sinks, and stoves. There were sewing machines and a headless, armless mannequin for making patterns and adjusting hems. Tucked in one corner of the room were a washer and dryer. They were going to be graded . . . *on laundry?* Payton laughed. "Well, it's not exactly the chemistry lab, is it?"

"Nope," Marley said, with a grin. "And Mrs. Crutchfield is, like, a hundred years old, so she doesn't even know what's going on most of the time. She was my *mom's* home ec teacher, and Mom says she wasn't young back then."

"She was my mom's home ec teacher, too," Payton said. "Mom said that when she was a freshman, girls were *required* to take home ec."

"Wow, that's super sexist," Marley said. "What did the boys do while the girls were taking home ec?"

"They took geography. Mom said it was like the school was saying that boys needed to know their way around the world, but girls just needed to know their way around the kitchen." Payton's mom did know her way around the kitchen, but she also knew her way around the bank where she was branch manager. Like her mom, Payton wanted a future where she could balance a career and a family.

"Good afternoon, young ladies," Payton and

Marley's conversation was interrupted by the quivery voice of Mrs. Crutchfield, who had just tottered into the room. She was a tiny, birdlike woman, wearing a navy-blue dotted dress that she could very well have worn back when she was Payton's mom's teacher. Or somebody's grandmother's teacher. "And welcome to home economics, where you will be learning the art of keeping a gracious home."

Payton rolled her eyes and gave Marley a look, which caused her to have to suppress a giggle. *Wait*, Peyton, thought. Mrs. Crutchfield had said *young ladies*. Did that mean there were no boys in the class? She looked around the room. Only girls. So maybe times hadn't changed that much since her mom was in school. Boys were allowed to take home ec now, but apparently they didn't choose to do so.

"You're going to learn skills such as cooking and cleaning and sewing," Mrs. Crutchfield said, gesturing toward the kitchen equipment and sewing machines in the room. "But you're also going to learn the almost-lost art of etiquette. Might any of you young ladies be able to use the word *etiquette* in a sentence?"

"I ate a kit—a Freddy Fazbear's Pizza Kit," Payton whispered to Marley, who laughed. Freddy Fazbear's Pizza Kits were all the rage, even among high school kids. It was a nostalgia thing, Payton supposed.

Whether it was for a birthday or for no particular reason, visiting the Freddy Fazbear's Pizza Kit Factory to build your own pizza was comforting . . . and delicious.

Mrs. Crutchfield turned her head toward Payton. "Could you repeat that so the whole class can hear it, please?"

Payton felt her face heating up. "It was just a stupid joke I whispered to Marley."

"Yes," Mrs. Crutchfield said. "And now I am asking you to share it with the whole class."

Payton knew her face was as red as a tomato. "I said, 'I ate a kit—a Freddy Fazbear's Pizza Kit.'"

A few kids tittered, but the pun didn't seem nearly as funny when she had to say it out loud for everyone to hear.

"Very amusing," Mrs. Crutchfield said. "And it's interesting that you mentioned Freddy Fazbear's Pizza Kits because next week we will be joining the culinary arts class for a visit to the factory where they are made."

The class erupted in cheers and cries of "Awesome!" and "Yesss!"

Mrs. Crutchfield displayed a very slight smile. "Permission slips will go out on Wednesday." She looked at Payton with a stern expression. "But now, in all seriousness, can you give the class a definition of the word *etiquette*?"

Payton was more than ready for Mrs. Crutchfield's attention to shift elsewhere. "Doesn't it mean, like, good manners?"

"Yes," Mrs. Crutchfield said. "And from now on, I ask you to demonstrate good manners by raising your hand before you speak in my class."

"Yes, ma'am," Payton said, barely above a whisper. She wondered if this class was going to be the walk in the park that Marley said it was. Mrs. Crutchfield might be old, but it didn't seem like she missed much.

"Hey, could you set the table while I get the spaghetti cooking?" Payton's mom said. She was still wearing her nice blue blouse and gray dress slacks from work, but she had taken off her pumps and replaced them with fuzzy pink house slippers.

"Sure," Payton said, getting up from the couch where she had been aimlessly channel surfing. "And thanks to Mrs. Crutchfield, I'll set the table one hundred percent correctly so everybody will know we're living in a"—she made quotation marks with the index and middle fingers of both hands—"*gracious home.*'"

Payton's mom laughed. "Yeah, a gracious home where spaghetti with jarred sauce and a bag of premade salad are on the dinner menu! Mrs. Crutchfield would probably call Child Protective Services if she knew what I'm feeding you." She dropped the contents of a box of spaghetti into a steaming pot of water. "How is Mrs. Crutchfield doing anyway? The woman has got to be older than dirt."

Payton opened the silverware drawer and retrieved three forks. "She still seems pretty sharp. She was sharp enough to call me out when I made a snarky comment to Marley."

"Yeah, you need to watch those," Mom said, stirring the noodles. "I made snarky comments when I was in her class, too, so she probably thinks you come by it honestly."

"Because I do," Payton said, smiling. She set the forks to the left of the plates. Mrs. Crutchfield said there should be separate forks for the salad and the entrée, but Payton put down one fork per plate only. Why wash more silverware?

"I still don't know why you let Marley talk you into taking that class," Mom said, stirring the sauce with a wooden spoon. "You could've taken art instead. You like art, and you're good at it."

"Are you implying that I'm not good at gracious homemaking?" Payton said, batting her eyelashes theatrically and doing a curtsy.

Mom smiled and shook her head. "I'm implying that from the look of your room, you don't care a fig about gracious homemaking. I'm also implying that sometimes you let Marley talk you into things you wouldn't do otherwise."

Payton sighed. It was an old argument. "You don't like Marley."

"I like Marley fine," Mom said, ripping open the bag of salad and dumping its contents into a bowl. "But she has a really strong personality and strong opinions, and I think that sometimes she steamrolls over other people and their wishes and opinions."

"She doesn't steamroll over me," Payton said, opening the fridge door to find the Parmesan cheese. *People did say that Marley is bossy, but that's just because she's a natural leader*, Payton thought.

"Really?" Mom raised an eyebrow. "So you're telling me you would've taken home ec even if Marley hadn't suggested it?"

Payton hated it when her mom backed her into a corner. Even when you were right, there was no winning an argument with her. *Now who's the steamroller?*

"No, I wouldn't have thought to take it. But the way she told me about it, it sounded fun and kind of . . . funny."

"Well, I hope you find it funny when Mrs. Crutchfield grades you on boiling an egg. And gives you a C minus. I'm speaking from experience here. The woman has impossible standards."

Payton sat on her bed, propped up on pillows, doing a boring social studies assignment on her laptop. On her walls, posters of the boys from her favorite K-pop group smiled down at her like they were inviting her to abandon her drudgery and go dancing with them instead.

An instant message from Marley popped up on her screen: "What are you doing?"

Payton welcomed the distraction. "Homework. You?"

"Nothing. Bored. You wanna go over to the Tastee Kone?"

"Doing homework. Remember?"

"So finish it or ditch it, who cares? I'll meet you on the corner of Brook and Branch in half an hour."

Payton hesitated before responding. If she were to meet Marley in half an hour, that would mean she'd just have twenty minutes to finish her homework, which wasn't a realistic amount of time for the assignment she had. But a chocolate-vanilla swirl cone would taste really good, and it was always fun to see who was hanging out at the Tastee Kone. Marley knew everybody and made easy conversation with them, unlike Payton, who tended to be on the shy side. But she felt less shy when she was with Marley. "Okay," she finally typed. "See you in thirty."

Payton raced through the rest of her homework assignment, doing what she knew was a slapdash job. When she came downstairs, her mom and dad were on the couch watching one of those crime shows they found endlessly entertaining, even though every episode seemed identical to Payton. "Hey," Payton said, already halfway to the front door, "I'm going to walk with Marley to the Tastee Kone."

"Did you finish your homework?" Mom asked.

"Yes," Payton said. She didn't do it well, but she did finish it.

"Do you need some money?" her dad asked.

"Got some. Thanks!"

As Payton shut the door behind her, she heard her mom call, "Be home by dark!"

Marley was standing on the corner of Brook and Branch, as promised. "I had to get out of the house," Marley said. "Mom and Dad have company—these friends they went to college with—and they're sooo boring! Every story starts with 'Do you remember that time . . . ?' and ends with something totally unmemorable."

Payton laughed. "Hey, at least they're trying to have fun."

"Trying but failing," Marley said. "It's pathetic. Do you think you get to be a certain age and then just automatically get boring?"

"I hope not," Payton said. It was upsetting to think about. One birthday too many, and then you were an adult and incapable of having fun. It was all the more reason to have as much fun as possible now.

They walked toward the Tastee Kone. A boy rode by on a bike and almost wrecked because he was looking at Marley.

It was impossible not to be aware of Marley's beauty. She had golden-blond hair and big blue eyes that somehow, unfairly, managed to have long dark, lashes. Her body was slim but curvy enough to be feminine. Boys tripped over their feet or over their words when confronted by her. Girls were either too jealous or too insecure to be Marley's friend, but not Payton. Payton had no illusions about her own looks. So far, her short, skinny body was so free of curves she looked like she'd been drawn using a ruler. Her hair and eyes were a dull brown, and she had freckles that she hated. But when she hung out with Marley, she felt like a little of Marley's glitter might rub off on her. She was like a plain little sparrow who was best friends with a flamingo.

Outside the Tastee Kone, they sat at a picnic table, Payton with a chocolate-vanilla swirl cone and Marley with a huge banana split. Another thing Payton had noticed was that Marley could eat whatever she wanted and never seemed to gain an ounce.

"Don't look at the table behind us," Marley whispered, spooning up ice cream with banana and chocolate sauce.

Naturally, Payton looked. It was a table full of boys who were in their history class, drinking milkshakes and trading insults and laughing the way boys did.

"I told you not to look!" Marley hissed at her.

"If you tell somebody not to look at something, they're automatically going to look," Payton said. "It's like in elementary school when somebody tells you not to do something, then you do it anyway and say it's Opposite Day."

Marley smiled. It was a dazzling smile even though there was hot fudge sauce on her upper lip. "Sean Anderson is sitting at that table," she whispered. "Emma Franklin said that Sean likes me."

Payton rolled her eyes. "Marley, it's not like that's newsworthy or anything. All the guys like you."

"That's not true!" Marley blushed, spooning up more ice cream. "Well, okay, *most* guys like me, but most guys are gross. Sean's not gross. He's on the Principal's List for good grades *and* he's on the basketball team, so he's well-rounded. Plus, he smells good."

"Well, not stinking is important." Payton said it to be funny, but it was true. A lot of ninth-grade boys were not yet on speaking terms with deodorant, a fact that made the school hallways smell like a giant armpit. "Why don't you go talk to him?"

"I can't just go talk to him!" Marley looked at Payton like she'd just said the most ridiculous thing on earth.

"Okay." Often Payton felt that there was some kind of script for male-female behavior that Marley had received but that she had missed out on. Payton tended to be straightforward with people, but apparently straightforwardness with the opposite sex violated some elaborate set of rules no one had ever bothered explaining to her.

"Well, I can't go talk to him alone," Marley said. "Maybe as we're leaving, we'll walk by his table. If he looks at me, I'll say hi to him. But it has to look casual, like I just happened to see him as we were leaving, not like I was going past his table to say hi to him on purpose."

"Okay," Payton said again. While hanging out with Marley, there was always so much drama; Payton sometimes felt like she was a minor character in a play Marley was starring in. Payton didn't feel like she knew all the lines for this play or even like she quite understood the plot, but it was still entertaining, and she was happy that a star like Marley had agreed to let Payton share the stage with her.

"Okay. Ready?" Marley asked as soon as Payton popped the last bite of cone into her mouth.

"Sure," Payton said, still chewing.

They got up from the table and threw away their trash, then walked past the table where the boys were sitting. Payton watched Marley work. Marley paused by the table just long enough to catch Sean's eye.

"Oh, hi, Sean," she said, as if she were surprised to see him there.

Payton noticed that Sean's ears turned red.

"Hi, Marley," Sean said without making eye contact.

Nobody said hi to Payton, nor did she expect them to. As she and Marley walked away, she heard the guys teasing Sean and laughing. "Oh, hi, Sean," one of them said in an exaggeratedly high feminine voice.

Marley smiled. "Well, that got his attention."

"I think you already had it," Payton said.

"Well, now he knows that I know, which is important."

Payton's grades in school were higher than Marley's, yet often in conversations with Marley, she felt like she was slow to catch on. "He knows that you know what?"

Marley let out an annoyed-sounding sigh. "He knows that *I know* that he likes me, you dork! How can somebody be so smart and so stupid at the same time?"

Payton smiled and shrugged. "I don't know—but with your looks and social skills and my book smarts, if you mixed us together, we'd make the perfect person!"

To Payton's relief, Marley smiled back. "We would, wouldn't we? We could take over the world!

Hey, I don't feel like going home yet. Why don't we walk down to the park?"

Payton looked up at the graying sky. "I don't know. I told Mom I'd be home by dark."

Marley smiled her charming smile and cocked her head like an adorable puppy. "Come on, we'll just stay ten minutes. It won't be full dark for another half an hour." She nudged Payton's shoulder. "We can go to the pond and feed the ducks."

Payton sighed. She had loved ducks ever since she was a little girl—the way they were so graceful in the water and so hilariously clumsy out of it. She loved their blank, serene little faces and their nasal-sounding quacks. "Okay, but just for ten minutes."

"It's a deal!" Marley said. "Come on, we'll have more time there if we run!"

Marley ran gracefully, and Payton jogged along behind her on her short little legs. *Like a greyhound being pursued by a corgi*, Payton thought.

Payton and Marley put quarters into the duck food dispensers. At the sound of the pellets pouring from the chute, the ducks swam toward them, then waddled onto land, shaking their wet tail feathers.

"Here you go, guys," Payton said, scattering the food on the ground. They bobbed their heads, quacking, and gobbled it up.

Marley said, "You want it? Go get it!" and tossed the food so the ducks had to waddle a long way to find it. Some of them weren't bright enough to track where the food had landed, and Marley laughed.

"You're making them work awfully hard for those pellets," Payton said, watching the confused ducks wander around.

"Hey, they should get some exercise," Marley said, grinning. "People feed them all day long. They're little fatties."

"They don't look that fat to me," Payton muttered to herself, but she let Marley have her fun. When the confused ducks finally wandered back her way, though, she made sure to place some food right in front of them.

The streetlights came on.

"Oh no," Payton said. "We've stayed here longer than ten minutes, haven't we? I've got to go. My mom's going to kill me."

Marley shook her head. "You are such a little rule follower. I guarantee your mom isn't going to kill you. She's probably just going to yell at you a little. And if she yells at you, so what?"

Payton knew Marley wouldn't understand, but the real answer to "so what?" was that Payton didn't like to disappoint her mom. She got along with her parents much better than most kids her age, and she wanted to keep it that way.

"Let's run!" Payton said.

They ran until they reached the corner of Brook

and Branch, where they stopped to part ways. "Thanks for helping me out with Sean tonight," Marley said, giving Payton a little half hug. "Tomorrow at lunch it's his turn to say hi to me. If he knows what he's doing. Which boys usually don't." Marley crinkled her nose thinking of it, then gave a little wave good-bye, and disappeared down her street.

It was definitely full dark. As she walked home, Payton tried to construct her side of the argument she knew she'd have with her mom as soon as she got home.

"Hi, Payton!" a voice called.

Payton looked over at the house two doors down from hers, where Abigail Sullivan was sitting on the front porch. *What kind of person sits on her front porch by herself in the dark?* Payton wondered. But then she remembered how weird Abigail was, which answered her question. "Hi, Abigail," Payton said, not stopping since she was already late.

Now Payton and Abigail had so little in common that it was strange to think they were once best friends. Because Abigail's house was so close to hers, the two of them had played together as preschoolers, playing dolls and store and school, wetting the sand in the sandbox to make castles and pies. They were inseparable when they started school and stayed that way until seventh grade, when Payton started being interested in more grown-up things and Abigail still wanted to play games and talk about wizards and unicorns. Payton had flung herself in the direction of the popular girls, who eventually accepted her. She had left Abigail to fend for herself. Sometimes from her spot at the popular girls' table in the school cafeteria Payton would see Abigail sitting alone reading a book.

"I know I'm late," Payton said as she walked in the front door. She figured she would cut her mom's accusation short by confessing up front.

"You are," her mom said. "I was about to ask your dad to drive around and look for you."

"Come on, I'm not *that* late," Payton said, flopping down on the couch. Her mom was such a worrywart. It was what came of watching all those crime shows on TV.

"You're late enough. I told you to be home before dark, and you're home after dark," her mom said. "Do I need to explain to you what *before* and *after* mean?"

Payton stifled the urge to roll her eyes. Her mother hated nothing more than an eye roll. "No, you don't need to explain what *before* and *after* mean."

"I'm glad to hear it." Her mom's voice was tight with tension. "You know, I never worried about you like this when you were hanging out with Abigail."

Payton was in no mood for one of her mom's

"Abigail good/Marley bad" lectures. "That was because Abigail lives just two doors down."

"No, it was because Abigail is responsible, and when you were with Abigail, I knew you'd be responsible, too. With Marley, I'm not so sure."

"When Abigail and I were best friends, we were little kids. It wasn't that we were so responsible; it was that an adult was watching us all the time. Marley and I aren't little kids. You haven't gotten used to the fact that I'm not a baby anymore."

Her mom sighed. "Payton, I'll still think of you as my baby even when you're thirty years old. I recognize that you're growing up, but part of growing up is showing responsibility. If you tell me you'll be home by a certain time, it's your responsibility to make that happen. If you want to be treated like an adult, you have to act like one."

The eye roll happened before Payton could stop it. But seriously, where had her mom gotten that statement? *The Parents' Big Book of Clichés?*

"Eye rolling—that's very adult," her mom said. "Go take a shower and get ready for bed."

Payton dragged herself up the stairs as slowly as she possibly could. She didn't want to push her luck anymore by being openly disobedient, but she also wanted her mom to know that she wasn't happy about following orders.

★ ★ ★

This week the unit they were studying in home ec was called "Eggs: The Basics." On Monday, Mrs. Crutchfield had lectured them on the nuances of shopping for eggs, which included the importance of checking for expiration dates and breakage. They had made both hard-boiled and soft-boiled eggs, which Payton thought was going to be the easiest cooking assignment ever. She was shocked when Mrs. Crutchfield gave her a B because she didn't wash the egg before boiling it. Seriously? It wasn't like you ate the shell, and besides, didn't boiling water clean things anyway?

At least Payton did better than her mom did when she was in Mrs. Crutchfield's class. Her mom had been a C-minus egg boiler.

Tuesday was scrambled eggs—a B plus because they were slightly overdone—and Wednesday was poached (a D plus, and a mess to boot). Payton was beginning to doubt that the course was going to be the easy A Marley had said it was.

Today, though, they were having a "break from eggs"—Mrs. Crutchfield laughed entirely too much when she said this—to go on their field trip to the Freddy Fazbear's Pizza Kit Factory where the pizza kits were made. Payton wasn't that excited about touring the factory, but she was definitely relieved to get away from all those eggs. On the tour, the kids would get to make their own pizza kits, which would be delivered to home ec class the next day. After days of eggs prepared in every way imaginable, a pizza sounded pretty good.

Payton took a seat next to Marley on the bus. The culinary arts class boarded after them, including Sean Anderson, who caught sight of Marley and promptly stumbled into the person in front of him. Marley and Payton laughed.

"He's trying to get up the nerve to ask me to the fall dance," Marley whispered after he was out of earshot.

"It would be easier if he didn't *fall* every time he saw you," Payton said, and they both giggled. Payton was glad she could make Marley laugh. She knew she couldn't be the pretty friend, but at least she could be the funny friend.

"This tour is gonna be lame," Marley said.

"So lame," Payton said, even though she was actually glad for the break in routine.

"Freddy Fazbear is for babies, and the sauce on Freddy's pizza tastes like ketchup. The crust is Styrofoam, and I don't even know what the cheese is made out of." Marley yawned, Payton supposed, to demonstrate that she was already bored with the experience even though it hadn't happened yet.

"Dandruff," Payton said. "The cheese is actually the dandruff of the Freddy Fazbear factory workers. They just shake their heads over every pizza."

"Eww, gross!" Marley said, but she was laughing.

When they got off the bus, Mrs. Crutchfield read their names from a clipboard and made them line up alphabetically. "Now in a moment, the factory manager, Ms. Bryant, is going to join us and tell you about the factory's safety regulations. Please play close attention. Factories are dangerous places if you don't follow the rules."

Marley rolled her eyes. "How dangerous could a pizza factory be?"

Payton didn't have time to think up a wisecrack because a pretty, short Black woman, presumably Ms. Bryant, came out to join Mrs. Crutchfield. Though the factory manager wore the same kind of net cap cafeteria workers wore on their heads, her body was encased in a yellow bird costume that looked like a Freddy Fazbear friend that Payton remembered from her childhood. The bird had always been Payton's favorite, and for a moment she racked her brain to remember its name. *Chica* . . . that was it. Payton smiled to see the Chica costume's familiar bib, neatly printed with the words LET'S EAT with the word PIZZA scribbled in marker below.

"Good morning, young ladies and gentlemen, and welcome to Freddy Fazbear's Pizza Kit factory!" the factory manager said, smiling. "We like to think we make the best custom pizzas in the country, and we're delighted to have you as our guests today. Now first things first, everybody's going to have to wear a fashionable cap like the one I have on here." She posed like a model and then laughed.

Marley let out a loud groan, and Mrs. Crutchfield shot her a look.

"I know they're not very glamorous, but it's a hygiene issue," Mrs. Bryant continued. "Nobody wants human hair as a pizza topping."

Now there were more groans, this time from disgust.

Ms. Bryant handed Mrs. Crutchfield a box. "Mrs. Crutchfield, if you would pass out the caps, please. Now, ladies and gentlemen, make sure all your hair gets tucked inside. Those of you with long hair need to be especially careful."

"This is already worse than I thought it would be," Marley said, holding her cap between her index finger and thumb as if it were a dead rat.

Payton put on her cap and tucked her hair inside. "I look like one of the old ladies who works in the school cafeteria," she said. She scrunched her face up into an old ladyish expression and said, "You want some corn with that?"

Marley shook her head. "You are such a dork." She slapped the cap onto her head. "My hair is going to be an ugly, sweaty mess by the time I get to take this thing off."

"Now let me continue to have your attention,

please," Mrs. Bryant said. "There are a number of safety rules for touring the facility. Walk in a straight line, and stay with your group at all times. There is to be no touching of any of the factory equipment under any circumstances. However"—she smiled—"each of you will be given a card and a pencil to carry with you as you tour the facility. Put your name on the card and check off the toppings you would like to have in your very own Freddy Fazbear's Pizza Kit. Each of your pizzas will be assembled and then delivered to you at your school tomorrow." She smiled widely. "How cool is that?"

No one offered an opinion on how cool it was.

"Oh, and one other thing," Ms. Bryant said. She sounded a little disappointed that people weren't acting more excited. "As you enter the facility, make sure you grab some earplugs from James, who's standing there by the door. It can get awfully loud in there!" She looked around, trying one more hopeful smile. "Well, be safe, and enjoy the tour. Shall we get started?"

Payton was surprised at how loud the inside of the factory was, even with her earplugs in. She couldn't imagine what it must be like to work in that level of noise all day. Ms. Bryant had to yell into a megaphone to make herself heard over the whirring and chugging of the machinery. "This first area is where the dough is mixed," she yelled.

Workers in caps, plastic gloves, and white smocks dumped flour and yeast and water into giant cannisters fitted with enormous metal blades that mixed the ingredients into a gooey, stretchy dough. "And the next room is where it gets kind of hot," Ms. Bryant said, leading them into a sauna-like room where huge vats of tomato sauce bubbled and steamed while being stirred by gigantic paddles. Even standing in the room for a minute made Payton break out in a sweat, and she wondered how the workers could stand the heat all day. The bubbling vats reminded her of witch's cauldrons.

"This is gross," Marley whispered. "It's so hot I already feel like I need a shower."

"And now if you'll follow me, you'll see where it all comes together," Ms. Bryant said, motioning them forward. "The assembly line. And here's where it gets really loud!"

The whirring, chugging, and pounding in the assembly room was almost too loud to bear. Ms. Bryant pointed out where the dough was dropped into balls, then flattened into disks. The disks moved forward on a conveyer belt and were then squirted with sauce. Next, the saucy dough was sprinkled with cheese.

"Next is what we call our topping bar," Ms. Bryant said, gesturing toward huge clear cylinders labeled PEPPERONI, SAUSAGE, PEPPERS, GROUND BEEF,

MEATBALLS, ANCHOVIES, MUSHROOMS, ONIONS, BLACK OLIVES, PINEAPPLE, ARTICHOKE, SPINACH, EGGPLANT. "Here, let's take a break. Feel free to fill out the cards choosing what toppings you want on your pizza kit."

Payton checked pepperoni and mushrooms. Not pineapple. Pineapple on pizza was an abomination. And did anybody really eat anchovies? An anchovy and pineapple pizza was the grossest combination she could imagine.

"If you're still undecided on what you want, hang on to your card. We'll collect the stragglers on the bus," Ms. Bryant said. "Next up is the pizza packaging center."

"Psst, Payton!" Marley muttered.

"What?" Payton said. She was actually enjoying the pizza tour more than she had thought she would.

"Let's go up those stairs." Marley cocked her head in the direction of a set of metal stairs leading up to some kind of catwalk. It was the type of staircase that had holes in the stairs so you could look through them and see how high you were off the ground. Payton didn't want to be reminded how far she was from the ground. She hated heights.

"I don't know," Payton said. "We're supposed to stay in line with the rest of the group."

"Come on, this tour is boring." Marley flashed

her most charming smile. "Let's explore. See what's up there."

"No, we'd better not," Payton said, but she could see that Marley had that look that meant she wouldn't take no for an answer.

Marley grabbed Payton's hand and pulled her. "Come on. We'll just go up for a minute and have a peek. Don't be such an old lady. You act like you're as ancient as Mrs. Crutchfield."

Payton didn't want to seem like Mrs. Crutchfield. She wanted to be young and have fun while she still could. She sighed. "Okay. But just for a minute."

Payton followed Marley up the rickety-seeming metal stairs, trying not to look down at her feet. Steam from the vats on the production line was rising, making it look like they were walking into a cloud. They stood together on the narrow catwalk. Marley was energetic and laughing, but Payton didn't like being there. The railings didn't seem high enough to be safe, and a sign reading FALL WARNING showed a stick man plummeting to his doom. It was unnerving. "Can we go back down now?" Payton asked. As was always the case when she was in a high place, her feet tingled and her stomach felt like it had migrated to the back of her throat.

"Not yet!" Marley said. "It's cool up here. All this steam makes it look like a horror movie where a monster comes out of the fog and"—Marley lunged toward Payton—"grabs you!"

Payton felt like her heart was going to thud out of her chest. She took a deep breath and tried to get ahold of herself. "Stop! You can't startle me like that. Not up here."

Marley looked at her, then grinned. "Hey, you're really scared, aren't you?"

"I don't like heights. Don't you remember how I wouldn't go on the Ferris wheel with you at the fair?" She had intended to go on the ride and had even stood in line with Marley, but had chickened out at the last minute.

"That's right. You stayed on the ground and just waved at me," Marley said. "Well, there's no reason to be scared up here. I'm sure this factory has safety regulations. I'm sure it's safe to run." She did a quick sprint down the catwalk, then ran back to where Payton was standing. "Or to jump up and down."

As Marley jumped, Payton could feel the catwalk give way a little. It made a horrible creaking sound. She grabbed on to the railing, afraid she might be sick. "Marley, please stop."

Marley laughed. "Why should I stop just because *you're* scared? I'm having an awesome time, and I'm sure everything's super safe." She looked at a sign reading DON'T LEAN ON THE RAILINGS. "I bet that's even safe." She leaned her back against one railing and then propelled herself forward to lean into the one on the opposite side of the walkway.

The railing wasn't safe.

Marley plunged forward and down, disappearing into the rising steam. Payton screamed, but the sound was drowned out by the whirring and grinding of the machinery below.

Her heart pounding, Payton ran down the stairs to look for her friend. She looked for Marley's injured body on the floor, but she was nowhere in sight. Payton looked at the steaming vats of sauce being constantly stirred by a giant metal paddle. How hot was that sauce? How deep was the vat? Could a person fall into it and—

She struggled with even thinking of the word *live*. But that was what she was asking, wasn't it? Could a person fall into one of those vats and live?

In her heart, she wanted to believe it was possible, but her brain told her differently.

She approached the two nearest vats and tried to sort out the sounds they were making from all the other sounds in the factory. Was it her imagination, or was one of them making a smooth sloshing sound, while the other one sounded more like *slosh, thump. Slosh, thump.* She stood and listened for a moment until the thumping stopped, maybe because it really did or maybe because it had been her imagination in the first place.

She didn't know where Marley was, but there was one thing she did know: If Marley had fallen into one of those vats, there was no way Payton could get her out.

Maybe if she told Mrs. Crutchfield, somebody could do something. But here, too, her heart and her brain told her something different. She wanted to believe that Marley could be okay, but the facts said otherwise: She had fallen from a good height. The vats of tomato sauce were boiling hot. Several minutes had passed since the accident, which meant it was probably too late.

Marley could feel a distant ringing in her ears, and her vision narrowed to a pinprick. Her parents' endless binge-watching of true crime shows told her that she was going into shock. Her mind whirled.

What if she told Mrs. Crutchfield, but the old woman said it was Payton's fault for not talking Marley down? Or what if one of her classmates accused Payton of *pushing* Marley in? Marley was beautiful and popular, it wouldn't be long before kids started to talk. Maybe they'd think Payton was jealous, and there had been no one there to see it beside Payton herself. As if a switch had flipped on, Payton felt herself going into self-preservation mode. It was too late to save Marley, but maybe she could at least save herself.

Up ahead, the members of her class were heading

toward the exit. If she just fell into line, maybe nobody would notice that she had wandered off for a few minutes.

She took a deep breath and went to join her classmates.

As they boarded the bus, Mrs. Crutchfield stood next to the door and checked students' names off her list. Payton had a sinking feeling in the pit of her stomach. She walked past Mrs. Crutchfield, boarded the bus, and took the same seat she had sat in on the way to the factory. It was glaringly obvious that the seat next to her was empty.

After everybody else had taken their seats, Mrs. Crutchfield tottered over toward Payton with a concerned look on her face. "Do you know where Marley is?" Mrs. Crutchfield asked, eyeing the empty seat.

"No, ma'am," Payton said. It wasn't quite a lie. Marley could be in any one of the vats; Payton didn't know which one.

Mrs. Crutchfield's eyes narrowed. "Weren't the two of you together on the tour?"

"We were for a while, but then we . . . got separated," Payton said. Once again, not really a lie. They got separated when Payton remained on the catwalk and Marley fell from it. "Marley said she thought the tour was boring. Maybe she just bailed and walked home."

"Without telling her best friend?" Mrs. Crutchfield asked.

"Well, you know Marley. She's pretty independent."

Mrs. Crutchfield was silent for a moment. "You have her phone number, I presume?"

"Yes I do, ma'am." Payton couldn't tell if Mrs. Crutchfield was really looking at her suspiciously or if she was just being paranoid.

Mrs. Crutchfield nodded. "Call her, please."

Payton's hand shook as she took out her phone and pulled up Marley's name on her contacts list. The phone didn't ring on Marley's end, probably because it had been cooked in a vat of tomato sauce.

Cooked in a vat of tomato sauce. Like Marley.

Payton had to swallow hard to keep from being sick. "No answer," she said.

Mrs. Crutchfield looked like she knew there was something Payton wasn't telling her. Payton figured Mrs. Crutchfield had been teaching far too long not to know when a kid wasn't being honest. Finally, thankfully, Mrs. Crutchfield broke eye contact. "Well, I guess I'll have to alert her parents," she said.

She turned and left. Payton was relieved not to feel her penetrating stare anymore.

But the relief didn't last. One look at the empty seat beside her was all it took for her panic to return.

★　★　★

When Payton walked into the house, her mom was on the phone. "Oh, here she is," she said. She held the phone out to Payton. "It's Marley's mom. She wants to talk to you."

Payton wanted to run, to go somewhere so far away that nobody could ask her any questions. But she held out her hand and took the phone. "Hello?" she said, her voice shaking.

"Payton, when was the last time you saw Marley?"

"Uh . . . she didn't come home?" Payton already felt like a liar. She knew Marley hadn't come home.

"If she had come home, I wouldn't be calling you!" Marley's mom's voice broke into a sob. "I'm sorry. That sounded rude. I'm just really upset."

"I know. Me too. Marley's my best friend." Payton wiped away a tear. "She sat with me on the bus on the field trip. We got separated on the tour of the factory."

Payton winced as she said it, thinking of the moment they got separated: when Payton stayed standing on the catwalk and Marley fell, disappearing into the clouds of steam. She felt guilty talking to Marley's mom, but not guilty enough to tell the whole truth.

"Where was she when you last saw her?"

Payton took a deep breath. Here comes the big lie, she thought. "She was in line behind me when we were looking at the big containers of pizza toppings, but the next time I looked behind me, she was gone. She said she was bored, so I thought maybe she bailed. She's done it before."

"You're right. That wouldn't be out of character for Marley," Marley's mom said. "Listen, if you remember any detail—any little thing that might help us find her—call me."

"I will," Payton said. She hit END on the phone, sank into an armchair, and sobbed.

Her mom appeared with a box of tissues and a glass of ice water. "Here, drink some water. It's easy to get dehydrated when you're upset."

Marley accepted some tissues and the glass of water, but her throat was so choked up it was hard to swallow.

"So she was just there behind you and then she was gone?" Mom asked.

Payton nodded.

Her mom sat down on the couch. "You don't think somebody could have . . . taken her, do you?"

"I don't think so," Payton said. "I mean, I didn't see anybody else around."

"I don't think so either, not when I'm being rational anyway. It's just that you see so much crazy stuff on the news nowadays, it's hard not to be paranoid," her mom said. "Gina—Marley's mom—said they've already called the police, but Marley hasn't been gone long enough to be declared officially missing. I imagine the police will question everybody who works at the factory to make sure there weren't any creeps lurking around."

Payton hoped nobody at the factory would get in trouble over Marley's disappearance. She felt a tug at her conscience telling her to come clean, but she had already lied to so many people today—Mrs. Crutchfield, Marley's mom, her own mom—that it was hard to imagine backtracking and telling the truth. If she was afraid of getting into trouble because she and Marley snuck off, it was nothing compared to the trouble she'd be in now.

"I think I'm still in shock," Payton said. This statement, at least, was wholly true.

Her mom reached out and patted her arm. "Of course you are. I'm upset, too."

"But you don't even like Marley."

"I don't dislike her. I just don't think she always makes the best choices," her mom said. "And I'm devastated for Gina. This situation is every parent's worst nightmare."

Payton thought about the pain Marley's parents and little brother must be in. But would the pain be lessened if Payton told the truth? At least if they had no clue about Marley, they could still hold out some hope. "I think I need to go for a walk. Try to clear my head a little," Payton said.

Her mom reached out, grabbed Payton's hand, and

squeezed it tight. "Given what's happened with Marley, I'm kind of afraid to let you out of my sight."

Payton needed to get out of the house and have a few minutes in which she didn't have to think frantically about what to say and what not to say. "I'm just going to walk around the block, Mom. Like I do almost every day."

Her mom let go of her hand. "Okay. But don't be gone long."

As soon as Payton was out the door, she took big gulps of fresh air to try to calm herself. *Maybe Marley didn't really fall in the vat*, she told herself. Maybe Marley was okay. Maybe she had fallen, then gotten right up and walked off and just hadn't made it back home yet.

But deep down, Payton knew Marley wasn't okay. Even if she had missed one of the vats, you couldn't fall from a height like that and be okay. At best, you'd have multiple broken bones. At worst . . .

Payton took another deep breath. She knew what the worst-case scenario was, and she was pretty sure it had been Marley's fate.

Payton walked around the block, taking deep breaths and trying to shake the tension out of her arms. She probably looked like a crazy person, but she didn't care. Maybe she was a crazy person. Or maybe she was turning into one. At some point, if she kept on telling lie after lie, would she be unable to distinguish lies from the truth?

She stopped at the corner of Brook and Branch where she had met Marley the week before. It had been such a normal night: an ice-cream cone, some whispering about boys, a walk to the duck pond. It all seemed so innocent and simple. It felt like those things had happened a lifetime ago.

But that had been Before, and now it was After. There was no way to bring the time Before back, so she kept on walking.

She walked past the houses and yards she walked past every day. Everything looked the same, but it wasn't and would never be again.

"Hey, Payton," a voice called as she neared her house.

Payton looked in the direction of the voice. Abigail was sitting in a wicker chair on her porch with a book in her lap and a glass of lemonade on the table beside her. As always, her mousy-brown hair was pulled back in a careless ponytail, and her glasses had slipped down on her nose. She was wearing yoga pants and a T-shirt that said SHH . . . I'M READING. She looked comfortable but also lonely somehow.

"Hey, Abigail." Usually Payton just said hey and kept on walking. Today she stopped. "What are you reading?"

Abigail looked a little surprised that Payton was

engaging her in conversation. "Oh. It's just a mystery. It's about this girl who goes missing. It's pretty good."

A missing girl. Great, Payton thought.

"You know . . . I don't read as much as I used to," Payton said.

When Payton and Abigail had been friends, they swapped books back and forth all the time. They had read together and talked about what they were reading. They had been a two-girl book club. But when the friendship with Marley started, there was so much real-life drama and intrigue that there had been no time for books. "Maybe," Payton said, "you could recommend some good ones to me. I miss . . . I miss reading."

She had almost said *I miss you* but stopped herself. It was true, though. She did miss Abigail. She had only just realized it. While the other girls Payton knew had changed a lot when they started high school, worrying about makeup and clothes and what other people thought of them, Abigail seemed the same as she ever was. It was kind of nice.

"Say . . ." Abigail set her book down on the table. "Would you like a glass of lemonade?"

Suddenly Payton realized she was very thirsty. "Yeah, a glass of lemonade would be great."

Abigail stood. "I'll be right back." She disappeared into the house.

She came back with a tall, sweating glass. Jack, her fat Siamese cat, followed her out the front door, rubbing against her legs. "You can come up on the porch," she said.

"Thanks."

Payton climbed the steps to the porch and accepted the glass of lemonade from Abigail. Jack butted Payton's legs with his head and she bent down to pet him.

"You remember Jack," Abigail said.

"Of course I remember Jack," Payton said, petting him under his chin. "He's unforgettable. I remember when he was a tiny kitten, but he's a big boy now."

"A big, fat boy," Abigail said. "But he still thinks he's a tiny kitten. Would you like to sit down?" The time they had spent apart was making their meeting strangely formal, like two people who had just met and were being careful not to offend each other.

"Sure. Thanks." Payton sat and sipped her lemonade. It was cold and tart and bracing, the way she liked it.

"I'm sorry about Marley," Abigail said.

"You know about that?" Payton said. The high school gossip machine worked fast, apparently.

"It was all over school this afternoon," Abigail said. "People said that when the bus came back from the home ec field trip, Marley wasn't on it."

"Yeah," Payton said. "It's weird. We were touring

the factory, and it was like she was just there, and then she wasn't." She didn't want to lie to Abigail now that they had just started talking again, so she decided to stick to statements that were technically the truth.

Abigail nodded. "You know, I've never really liked Marley, but I wouldn't want something bad to happen to her. And that's what people are saying . . . that something bad happened. This afternoon somebody said that one of the kids on the field trip said they heard a scream."

Payton swallowed hard. Had Marley screamed as she fell? And if so, would it have been possible for someone to hear her over the noise of the factory's machinery? Everything that happened surrounding the accident was such a blur. Payton could remember rejoining the group, mindlessly filling out her pizza order card and turning it in, then sitting on the bus next to a conspicuously empty seat. The whole experience was as hazy in her mind as a dream.

"I want you to know," Abigail said, "that even though I dislike Marley, I don't wish her ill. I genuinely hope she's okay."

"You're jealous of Marley, aren't you?" Payton asked. She realized, with some embarrassment, that she hadn't spent much time thinking about Abigail's feelings.

"Oh, do you think?" Abigail sounded irritated. "I was your best friend, and you ditched me to be best friends with her. How could I not be jealous?"

Payton couldn't meet Abigail's eyes. "I didn't really ditch you. We just . . . grew apart."

"Well then, we grew apart very suddenly so you could be Marley's best friend instead. You really hurt my feelings, Payton."

Payton felt a sharp pain in her heart, like a bee had stung her there. "I'm sorry."

There was a long pause, and Abigail seemed to let out a breath she'd been holding this whole time. "It's okay. I forgive you."

"Thank you." Payton was glad she could be forgiven of this, at least.

"And I hope Marley's okay and I understand that she's your best friend now, but you know, sometimes maybe you and I could, you know, hang out."

"We're hanging out now," Payton said, letting herself smile a little.

Abigail smiled back. "Yeah, but this is our first time hanging out since you ditched me, so it's super awkward."

All the things Payton liked about Abigail came flooding back to her in a rush: her sense of humor, her intelligence, her honesty. She laughed. "It is! It's sooo awkward!"

Payton saw her mom walking down the sidewalk, a panicked look on her face. "Mom!" Payton called. "Hey, Mom! I'm over here!"

Payton's mom put her hand to her chest and let out a sigh of relief. "There you are. Good. I thought you'd just be gone for twenty minutes or so, but it's been almost an hour. I was worried about you because, well, you know . . ."

She didn't have to finish. "I'm sorry, Mom," Payton said. "I didn't mean to worry you."

"It's okay," her mom said, then looked at Abigail. "Hi, Abigail. It's nice to see you."

"It's nice to see you, too, Mrs. Thompson."

"You should come on home, though, Payton," her mom said. "Dinner's almost ready."

Payton stood up. "Okay." She turned to Abigail. "Let's hang out soon."

"Definitely," Abigail said. "And let me know if you hear anything about Marley."

Payton felt a stab of guilt that was becoming very familiar. "I will."

Payton sat down at the dinner table with her mom and dad like she did every night. Tonight they were having roasted chicken and rice and broccoli, all of which she liked well enough. But when she put a chunk of chicken in her mouth and tried to chew it, it tasted like dust. She knew there was no way she could swallow it, so she spat it into her napkin and hoped nobody noticed.

"I know it's been a tough day, honey, but you

should eat to keep your strength up," her mom said.

So much for nobody noticing.

"I can't," Payton said, pushing away her plate. "I mean, how can life go on as normal when something so bad has happened? How can people just go on eating dinner and doing homework and brushing their teeth and going to bed like everything's fine?"

"It's a good question," her dad said, looking thoughtful. "I guess people go on doing normal things because it's the only thing they *can* do—just go on living and hope things get better, which they generally will, over time."

Payton burst into tears. Things would never get better for Marley. And it would be a long, long time until things got better for Marley's parents and brother. "But what if they don't?" she said, sobbing. "What if they never do?"

Payton's mom and dad looked at each other the way they did when she asked a question they couldn't answer.

Payton didn't give them time to come up with anything. She knew they had no answers. No one did. She stood up. "May I be excused, please?"

"Sure, honey," her mom said. "But later you're going to eat something before you go to bed. Mom's orders."

Payton climbed the stairs to her room, flopped down on her bed, and cried some more. Apparently, she carried an endless well of tears inside her. She couldn't believe she hadn't run out of them by now. Today had been the hardest day of her life.

The only tiny bright spot was her talk with Abigail. She was glad the ice between them was thawing. She had forgotten how easy Abigail was to talk to, how natural things felt between them. It was a different dynamic from Payton's friendship with Marley. Payton was always trying to impress Marley, to win her approval, so she was always a little on edge around her. She knew Abigail accepted her as she was, so when she was with Abigail, she could just be herself.

Still, Payton wished more than anything that she could see Marley again, that she could hear Marley laugh and call her a dork because of some stupid joke she had made.

After a long cry, Payton took out her homework and tried to get started on it, but it was useless. What was the point of doing homework when people you loved could just disappear in the blink of an eye? Making an effort of any kind seemed pointless.

There was a light knock on the door. "Can I come in?" her mom asked.

"I guess so," Payton mumbled into her pillow.

Her mom was carrying a tray from which sweet and spicy smells emanated. "Hey, I made you some hot chocolate and cinnamon toast. I figured you

might be able to eat it when you couldn't eat anything else."

Cinnamon toast and hot chocolate had always
been Payton's go-to comfort foods when she was
sick or sad. Her mom had been making it for her
since she was a toddler. Payton sat up in bed.
"Thanks."

Her mother's kindness made her cry a little more.
Especially when she thought about how she was lying
to her mom about Marley.

"You're welcome." Her mom handed Payton a
saucer holding the slice of cinnamon toast and set the
mug of hot chocolate on the bedside table.

"I think I'd like to be left alone now if that's okay,"
Payton said. Looking at her mom's face made her feel
too guilty.

"Not until I've seen you eat at least half that
cinnamon toast," her mom said, sitting down on the
foot of the bed.

"Okay." Payton nibbled the cinnamon toast and
took a sip of hot chocolate. It was strange how
these things could still taste good even when life was
so bad.

"I've never had anything happen to me like what
happened to you today," her mom said. "It's hard
when you're the parent and you can't think of anything to say to make your kid feel better." Her mom
looked like she was in danger of crying herself. "I

guess all I can say is that your dad and I are here when you need us."

Payton nodded, too full of emotion to speak.

"Now, were you able to do your homework?" her mom asked.

Payton shook her head.

"How about I write your teachers a note? They'll know what happened, and they know Marley is your best friend. I bet they'll let you turn it in on Monday. And who knows? By then, Marley may be back at home safe and sound." She patted Payton's leg and got up from the bed.

"Thanks, Mom," Payton said, even as she knew Marley was neither safe nor sound.

Payton brushed her teeth, climbed into bed, and curled up in a little ball. She was sure she wouldn't be able to sleep, but the exhaustion of the day had been too much for her, and she lost consciousness as though she'd experienced a physical trauma, not just an emotional one.

She was surrounded by the whirring and churning of machinery. She looked around and saw she was in Freddy Fazbear's Pizza Kit factory. She was alone. She had gotten separated from her group, and she needed to find them. She entered a dimly lit room where vats of tomato sauce gurgled as they bubbled and boiled. She looked around frantically for any sign of her classmates or teacher. There was no one.

On the floor in front of the vats was a big black pot like a witch's cauldron. It was hanging over an open fire that had been built with some logs. An open fire inside a building? *Payton thought.* How is that even safe?

A familiar figure from Payton's early childhood walked out and took his place behind the cauldron. It was big, furry Freddy Fazbear with his tiny top hat and familiar grin. Freddy was carrying a big burlap bag, the kind that Christmas cards always showed Santa carrying. Humming to himself, Freddy reached into his bag and pulled out a long-handled wooden spoon. He dipped the spoon into the cauldron of sauce and then stirred. He dipped up a spoonful of sauce, sniffed it, then tasted it thoughtfully.

Freddy reached back into his bag and pulled out a human arm, pale and thin. He dropped it into the pot of sauce and stirred. He dipped into the bag and pulled out a foot next—a girl's foot, small with the toenails painted baby pink. He dropped it, too, into the bubbling cauldron.

Horror was building in Payton. Horror but also comprehension.

She was terrified of what he was going to pull out next, but she couldn't look away.

Freddy reached into the bag one more time and retrieved a severed head that he held by its luxurious blond hair. At first Payton couldn't see the face, but as Freddy turned the head around, she saw it was Marley, her eyes wide and unseeing, her mouth open in a silent scream. Freddy let go of the hair, and the head landed in the cauldron of sauce with a splash.

Payton woke up, gasping for breath. There would be no more sleeping tonight.

"I heard she ran away," one girl said to another standing in front of the lockers.

"I heard she ran off with Sean Anderson," the other girl said. "But that can't be right because Sean's at school today."

"I heard she ran off to New York City to be a model," a girl who had been listening in on the conversation weighed in.

The gossip buzzed in Payton's ears. Her head felt like a hive of angry bees. She sat in her math class, but she couldn't concentrate.

A voice came on over the intercom. "Payton Thompson, please report to the front office."

Payton felt a knot of fear form in her stomach. Whatever this was, it couldn't be good. Like a prisoner awaiting her sentence, she rose from her desk and walked to the office, consumed with dread.

When she reached the office, she wasn't comforted by the sight of a police officer standing by the front desk with her mom right beside him.

Payton's mind buzzed with panicked questions: Did the police know she was lying? Had they told her mom? Could a person get arrested for lying?

"Hey," her mom said. Payton could tell she was trying to sound casual, but the tone of her voice was strained, and her brow was wrinkled like it got when she was worried or upset. "Officer Jacobs wants to ask you a few questions since you seem to be the last person who saw Marley."

Payton shifted from foot to foot. She couldn't meet her mom's eyes, let alone the police officer's. "I don't know if I was the *last* person who saw her."

"Well, the other kids all seem to have lost track of her in the factory sooner than you did," her mom said, her voice getting shakier with each word. "And apparently nobody working in the factory says they saw a girl who got separated from the field trip group."

"I won't take up much of your time, and then you can get back to class," Officer Jacobs said. He was a large, bald man with a gentle face. Under other circumstances, Payton wouldn't have been scared of him. Officer Jacobs looked over at the secretary behind the front desk. "Ma'am, is there someplace private we could sit down and talk?"

The secretary stood up. "Of course. Let me show you to the conference room."

Payton sat in the small room beside her mom and across from Officer Jacobs. She felt like she was on one of those crime dramas her mom watched all the time. She wondered if her mom found this kind of drama less entertaining when it was in real life.

"So you rode the bus with Marley on the field

trip?" the officer asked, his pen poised above a notepad.

"Yes, sir," Payton said. She felt sweaty and wondered if it was noticeable. "We rode together on the way to the factory."

Officer Jacobs nodded. "And then you were together for the tour?"

"For part of it, yes. But it was like we were together and then we weren't."

It's not a lie, Payton told herself.

Officer Jacobs wrote something down. "And where were you in the process of touring the factory when you noticed Marley was missing?"

Payton started to sweat more profusely. What had she told her parents when they had asked her this question? The containers of pizza toppings. She was pretty sure she had told them they'd been near the containers of pizza toppings.

Previous to this experience, Payton had not been in the habit of telling lies. She was discovering how hard it was. Once you came up with a story, you had to stick with it regardless of whom you were talking to. It wasn't easy to remember the details and use them consistently. "Um . . . we were near the containers of pizza toppings, I think," Payton said.

"That was when you noticed she wasn't there?" the officer said.

"Yes, sir. I turned around, and she was gone."

The officer jotted something else down on his notepad. Payton wished she could see what he was writing. She feared it was the word *LIAR*.

The officer looked up from his notepad. "Had she said anything to you about leaving or maybe about having plans to meet someone later?"

"No, sir." Payton reconsidered. "Well, she didn't say anything about meeting anybody or anything like that, but she did say the tour was lame and a waste of time. So I figured maybe she just left."

The officer raised an eyebrow. "Without saying goodbye to her best friend?"

"Well, that's not what Marley's like. She does what she wants when she wants. If she got bored and decided she was going to go, she would've just gone. She's done it before."

The officer jotted something else down. "Well, thank you for your time. We'll be in touch if we need to ask you anything else. We're working very hard to find your friend."

"Okay, that's good," Payton said, but she knew it didn't sound like the right thing to say. It was hard to sound hopeful about their efforts when she knew good and well that there was no chance that they were going to find Marley alive. "Can I go back to class now?"

The officer nodded. As they left the conference room, Payton's mom put her arm around her shoulders. "I know that was hard. I'm proud of you. Are you going to be okay for the rest of the day?"

Payton nodded, but tears sprang to her eyes. She knew her mom wouldn't be proud of her if she knew the truth.

"It'll be okay," her mom said, giving her a little squeeze. "I just have a feeling you're going to be seeing your friend again real soon."

In home ec class, Mrs. Crutchfield stood next to a table stacked high with pizza boxes. "As you can see, our Freddy Fazbear Pizza Kits have been delivered," she said, looking around at the class. "Each pizza box has a student's name on it. When I call your name, come get your pizza kit. In order to save time, I took the liberty of preheating all the ovens to four hundred and twenty-five degrees. Bake your pizza for twelve to fourteen minutes according to the directions on the box, and then . . . *bon appétit!*" She picked up a pizza box and said, "Emma?"

Emma came to claim her pizza kit, and Mrs. Crutchfield continued calling the students' names. One by one, the girls shuffled to the front of the room to get their pizza creations.

When a girl named Hannah came up to get hers, she asked, "Mrs. Crutchfield, is there a pizza kit with Marley's name on it?"

"No, dear, I'm afraid not," Mrs. Crutchfield said,

not meeting Hannah's eyes. "Sadly, Marley disappeared before she could choose the ingredients for her pizza kit. But the police are looking for her, and I'm sure they'll find her safe and sound." Despite the reassuring words, Mrs. Crutchfield's tone did not sound confident. She picked up another pizza box. "Payton?" she called.

Payton got up from her seat next to the one Marley used to occupy. She walked to the front of the room and claimed her pizza kit. The box was white with red letters spelling out FREDDY FAZBEAR'S PIZZA KIT with a picture of Freddy smiling the same way he had in Payton's dream the night before. The box was soggy on the bottom, and when she pulled her hand away, it was red with what she hoped with all her heart was tomato sauce.

Of course it's tomato sauce, she told herself. *What else would it be?*

Tomato sauce. She thought of the big, steaming vats of tomato sauce where Marley had in all likelihood met her doom. Which would happen first if you fell into a vat like that: Would you drown or be boiled alive, or would you be beaten to death by the giant, always-turning paddles that stirred the sauce?

She lifted her fingers to her nose and sniffed them to make sure the red liquid had tomato sauce's familiar tang.

The smell of blood also had a tang.

Stop it, Payton told herself. *You're freaking out. If people see you freak out, they'll get suspicious. They'll know.*

"Payton, are you all right?"

Mrs. Crutchfield's voice penetrated Payton's racing mind. "What? Oh yes, Mrs. Crutchfield."

"Then please take your seat until the other girls have picked up their pizza kits."

"Yes, ma'am." Payton quickly sat down. She had no idea how long she'd been standing at the front of the classroom, lost in her panicky thoughts.

All around, her classmates were opening their pizza kits, oohing and aahing over them as if they were presents on Christmas morning. Their comments all blurred together in Payton's confused, frightened brain.

"Hey, this looks pretty good!"

"Looks way better than the mystery nuggets the cafeteria is serving for lunch today."

"Sausage and mushroom with extra cheese—my favorite! They weren't stingy with the extra cheese either."

With shaking hands, Payton opened her own pizza kit.

She looked down at the box's contents. Something about it didn't feel right.

Red liquid pooled in the bottom of the box. The

crust was not the usual pale color of dough but closer to the color of a bandage's approximation of Caucasian skin. With one trembling finger, she reached out and touched one of the pepperoni slices. It was soft and smooth. That wasn't how pepperoni usually felt, was it?

She thought of the game played in the dark at Halloween parties where you passed around the peeled grapes and said *These are the dead man's eyes*, then the cold spaghetti noodles: *These are the dead man's guts* . . .

Payton felt her stomach roil with nausea and her mouth fill with saliva. She couldn't be sick. If she got sick, it would call attention to her and make people think she knew more than she was saying. She swallowed hard, fighting her body's strong urge to vomit.

She would not be sick. She would not call attention to herself. She would bake her pizza and eat it just like everybody else. The thought of eating the pizza filled her with a disgust more intense than any feeling she had ever known in her life. But she was going to do it. She had to do it.

In the kitchen area, she took the soggy, dripping pizza from the box and slid it into the oven next to the other girls' pizzas.

Drops of red liquid fell from her pizza and splattered on the clean white floor.

"Whoa, Payton, you went a little heavy on the red sauce, didn't you?" Hannah said.

Payton forced a smile and shrugged. "What can I say? It's my favorite part." She grabbed a paper towel and wiped up the mess.

The other girls waited happily for their pizzas, talking about how they were starving and couldn't wait to eat them. Payton waited with a growing sense of dread. She hoped desperately that someone would pull a fire alarm, and by the time they returned to the classroom, the pizzas would be burnt and inedible. Or maybe she could drop hers on the floor so she wouldn't have to eat it.

No. Dropping it would make everybody look closely at her and closely at the pizza. They would know there was something wrong with her and something wrong with it.

When the bell on the oven timer rang, Payton jumped like a bomb had exploded.

There was no avoiding it. It was pizza time. As Mrs. Crutchfield had said, *Bon appétit.*

With shaking hands, Payton took her pizza out of the oven. She took out the pizza cutter and held it over the hot pie, feeling like she was wielding a deadly weapon. The sound of the sharp metal wheel slicing through the cheese and sauce and separating the crust into quarters was like a machete slicing through flesh.

All around her, girls exclaimed over their pizzas:
"It smells so good!"

"I want to take a bite right now, but I don't want
to burn my mouth!"

"The cheese is so gooey and stretchy!"

Payton picked up her pizza and carried it to her
table. She sat down and stared at it. The sauce was
bloodred. She poked the dough with her finger. It
was soft and somehow *fleshy*. The pepperoni
reminded her of a tongue.

The girls at the other tables were gobbling their
pizza slices, laughing and having a great time.

Payton stared down at the unappetizing pizza.
The pizza was evidence of how she had abandoned
Marley. Abandoned her and then lied about it.

Payton had no choice. She had to destroy the
evidence.

She had to eat it.

She swallowed hard to force down the lump that
had formed in her throat. She picked up the first slice
and took a tiny nibble from the tip of the triangle. It
tasted salty and greasy and metallic and *wrong*
somehow.

The texture of the dough was different than any
pizza she had ever eaten before. Fatty. Gristly. How
could dough be gristly?

She chewed and chewed, but somehow the food
didn't seem to be breaking down the way it should. It

almost seemed like it was growing bigger in her mouth instead of smaller. With great effort, she forced herself to swallow and felt the solid doughy ball work its way with difficulty down her esophagus toward her stomach. She was reminded of a nature documentary she saw once that showed a large boa constrictor eating a rat whole: You could see the shape of the unfortunate rodent as the snake's muscles forced it through its throat and into its belly.

The difference was that the snake appeared to be enjoying the rat way more than she was enjoying this pizza.

But there was no choice. She had to take another bite. And another. Each one was worse than the one before. Now that it was cooked, the pepperoni had the texture of peeling sunburned skin, and the sauce had a coppery tang like once when Payton had cut her finger and stuck it in her mouth.

She couldn't let thoughts like this flood her mind. Not if she was going to finish this pizza. She tried to take bigger bites to make it go faster, but it soon became apparent that this wasn't a good idea. The big chunks landed in her stomach as heavy as rocks, and when she looked at the pizza on her plate, it didn't look significantly smaller.

One slice. Most of the other girls had finished their pizzas and were washing their plates at the kitchen station, chatting and laughing. Payton had only made it through one slice. Eating this pizza was like swallowing stones.

"Are you all right, Payton?"

Payton looked up to see Mrs. Crutchfield standing beside her table, looking at her with a concerned expression.

"I beg your pardon?" Payton said. It was hard to talk. The last bite she took of the pizza still hung in her throat.

"I was asking if you're all right," Mrs. Crutchfield said. "You look pale."

"I'm fine," Payton said, though of course she wasn't.

Mrs. Crutchfield looked down at Payton's mostly uneaten pizza. "Do you not like what you made?"

"Oh, I like it. It's just very . . . filling."

Mrs. Crutchfield looked at her for a moment. "I know it must be hard on you with Marley missing. But I'm sure she'll turn up soon."

She's right here, Payton thought. *Right here on my plate.*

For a second, she thought she might actually laugh. She feared she was losing her mind.

But she nodded and said, "Thank you, ma'am. I hope so."

Payton was forcing down the last bite of pizza when the bell rang to change classes. She felt ill and bloated, as if the dough were expanding in her stomach, as if it might keep on expanding and expanding until she burst like a blood-filled tick.

She suffered through the last class of the day, her stomach churning, and then suffered even more on the bus ride home, as every bump and pothole the bus drove over made the unstable contents of her stomach threaten to evacuate the premises.

She stumbled through the front door of the house. "Hey, hon," her mom called from the kitchen. "Any word on Marley?"

Payton could barely get out the word *no*.

Her mom appeared in the living room and looked at her with a knitted brow. "Are you okay, sweetie? You don't look so good."

"Sick," Payton managed to get out with great effort. "Something I ate."

"Oh, that's too bad," Mom said. "And I'm sure worrying about Marley isn't helping any. I hope you feel better by dinnertime. I'm making pot roast. Your favorite."

Her mom's pot roast usually was her favorite, but now the thought of it sickened her. The stringy meat, stewed in its own fat and juices. Even the carrots and onions and potatoes were saturated in the juices of dead cow. First came death, then the butchering, then the cooking and eating of the flesh. Payton feared that the Freddy Fazbear's Pizza Kit had been her last experience eating the meat of another creature. From now on, assuming she could ever bring herself to eat anything again, she would be a vegetarian.

Payton remembered a vegetarian kid in middle school who used to wear a T-shirt with pictures of animals on it that said DON'T EAT YOUR FRIENDS. After today, these words had taken on a new meaning.

"Maybe you should take an antacid and go lie down," her mom said.

Payton nodded and dragged herself up the stairs to her room. She didn't take an antacid because she didn't think she could swallow anything and keep it down, not even medicine. She curled up on her bed and moaned softly in misery, drifting in and out of consciousness.

Payton's stomach churned. She had experienced indigestion and stomach viruses in the past, but never had her digestive system made this much noise. It rumbled, then sloshed, then gurgled so loudly that if anyone had been in the room with her, they would've heard it and asked what was wrong.

Maybe lying curled up on her side wasn't the best choice, she thought. Maybe it would be better to stretch out so her stomach wouldn't be so smooshed. She lay on her back. A wave of nausea washed over her, followed by sharp, almost unbearable pangs. Without really meaning to, she put her hands on her stomach. Something from inside her body bumped up against her palms like it was trying to push its way out.

What was it? It was horrible.

Payton lifted her shirt so she could see her belly. Usually flat, now it was expanding and contracting in a way she wasn't controlling. It felt like something was beating her up from the inside, punching her stomach so hard it was going to leave bruises.

This was not a normal stomachache. There was something inside her, something other than the disgusting pizza she had barely choked down in home ec class.

Payton had once watched a gross TV show about people infested with parasites. There had been a woman on the show who had had a giant tapeworm living in her stomach. The woman ate and ate but kept getting thinner because the tapeworm devoured everything she consumed. Finally, the woman learned that sometimes if you left a piece of food on your tongue, the tapeworm would crawl up to get it and then could be pulled out of your body. The woman had set a piece of raw steak on her tongue, and the tapeworm had crawled out of her stomach, up her esophagus, and into her mouth. When she pulled it out, it was eight feet long. Payton remembered that the woman had kept the deceased tapeworm in a jar on her mantel, which did not strike Payton as a sound decorating choice.

When she was thinking clearly, it really made no sense for her to believe that the pizza she had eaten had contained pieces of Marley. However, wasn't it possible that she had swallowed a worm? People ingested parasites all the time. If they didn't, why would there be a TV show about it? Maybe that was what had made her so sick. She wondered, if she put a piece of food on her tongue, would whatever was inside her crawl up to get it?

Her stomach churned harder and faster. Her belly expanded, swelling like a balloon. She could feel her skin stretch to its limit. Her body was definitely try-ing to expel something. It was time to take action.

Payton tiptoed downstairs. The TV was blaring one of her parents' crime shows, so she figured she could sneak into the kitchen undetected. She opened the refrigerator door and tried to decide on the best bait for luring a worm. There was no raw steak, but there was raw hamburger. She liked her burgers well done, so her stomach churned even harder as she thought of holding the cold, bloody beef on her tongue. Still, if doing so got rid of whatever was causing her such misery, it was worth the "ick" factor. It was amazing what a person was willing to do if they were desperate.

She pinched off a piece of the meat, rolled it into a small ball, palmed it, and headed back upstairs.

"Are you okay, Payton?" her mom called from the living room.

"Yeah, just got some ginger ale to settle my stomach," she called back, trying to sound as normal as possible.

"Good idea!" her mom said. "Let me know if you need anything, okay?"

Payton didn't know if what she was about to do was really a good idea. But she had to do something.

She sat down on the bed and placed the ball of raw ground beef on her tongue. It was clammy, with the metallic taste of blood. As her body temperature warmed the clump of meat, it started to secrete its juices, the blood and grease running down her throat. She didn't want to swallow it, but she didn't want it back in her mouth either. She gagged violently, and bitter saliva combined with the meat juices in her mouth, filling it with a sickening mixture of fluids.

She jumped up and ran to the bathroom, knowing that at the very least she was going to throw up. But maybe that was all she needed to do, she told herself. Throwing up was awful, but sometimes when something made you sick and you threw it up, you felt better afterward. Maybe that's all that would happen, she told herself.

But she knew she was telling herself a lie.

She winced at her reflection in the bathroom mirror. She was pale and sweaty. Her skin had a strange grayish cast, and there were dark half-moons under her eyes. She could never remember looking this bad. Maybe this illness was too serious to take care of at home. Maybe she should tell her mom she needed to go to the hospital to have her stomach pumped.

But if she told her mom about the pizza kit, would she also have to tell her she knew what happened to Marley? Would she have to admit that she had lied to a police officer? She was afraid that if she started talking, she wouldn't be able to stop, and all her secrets would spill out. She couldn't take the risk of getting into that much trouble.

So she waited. She opened her mouth wide, looking in the mirror, waiting for whatever it was to appear. She could see past her tongue to her uvula and into the dark tunnel of her throat. Holding her mouth open made the urge to gag stronger, especially as the now tepid raw meat continued to ooze. The meat's greasy fluids pooled underneath her tongue. It was repulsive. She couldn't stop thinking that what she was holding in her mouth was a chunk of mutilated dead cow. If she made it through this experience, she was definitely becoming a vegetarian.

The wait was excruciating. How long had it been? Minutes? Hours? It felt like it had been years and years.

There was a slight movement in her abdomen.

Was it the worm—or whatever it was—sensing the ground beef, sniffing it (if worms could smell), and starting to make its way toward it? But then it was still again. Had she only imagined it?

She waited some more, sickly saliva pooling in her mouth. She desperately wanted to spit the meat into the sink, but she knew it was her best chance at solving this problem on her own.

And then she felt it.

Something was moving in her stomach. It felt like it was uncoiling like a snake. She could feel the worm—if that's what it was—pushing itself out of her stomach and up her esophagus, but it was a different sensation than throwing up. The thing making its way up her torso was solid and slow.

And then she was choking. Coughing and retching, she looked in the mirror. Her throat was visibly pulsing as the thing inside her moved up the length of her neck. The words *better out than in* popped into her head, but in this case, she couldn't be sure they were true. She didn't want the thing to stay inside her, but she was also afraid to see it.

Her mouth popped open extra wide, like when the dentist pried it apart to fit in his tools. She looked at her gaping mouth in the mirror. She felt something wiggly against her palate. She leaned closer to the mirror to see better, then blinked and shook her head because she couldn't believe what she saw.

Fingers. Moving fingers with petal-pink polish— *Marley's color*—on the nails. The fingers were attached to a hand that she could see emerging from her stretched-out throat.

No no no no no. She couldn't let whatever that hand was attached to come out where she could see it. She reached in her mouth, grabbed the hand, and tried to shove it back into her esophagus. She swallowed as she shoved, trying to force it down. But the hand was too large, and it kept moving, kept pushing her hand away, like it was fighting her.

Payton gagged. Her body was trying to force out the very thing she was trying to force back in. She doubled over, heaving and sputtering. When she stood back up, her mouth stretched open so wide that her lips cracked and bled. The hand shot out of her mouth, its fingers blindly reaching and grabbing. In the mirror, Payton saw herself, her jaws wrenched open like a snake swallowing a whole rat, except it was a girl's hand and wrist, not a rat's tail, that protruded from her face.

Her airway blocked by the emerging arm, Payton wanted to breathe. She wanted to scream.

Certain she was going to suffocate if she didn't get help, she took a shaky step toward the bathroom door. So fast that she couldn't even process it, the hand retreated back into her mouth and down her throat, into her body cavity. Payton sucked in huge gasps of air and sank into a sitting position on the bathroom floor, too drained to make it back to her bedroom. She leaned against the white tile wall and spat the raw meat ball into a wad of toilet paper. She used a bath towel to wipe the cold sweat from her face.

She tried to process what had just happened. It definitely wasn't a worm that was inside her. There was no doubt in her mind that the hand that had shot out of her mouth was Marley's. She and Marley had done each other's nails at sleepovers. She knew her best friend's hand when she saw it.

Her best friend. Marley was her best friend, and she hadn't told anyone about her accident because she was afraid of getting in trouble. Maybe if she had told someone—Mrs. Crutchfield, one of the factory workers—they could have found Marley in time to save her. And even if it had been too late, at least that way Marley's parents would have known what happened to her. They wouldn't still be waiting and worrying.

But was Marley still alive? It had been her hand, and it was moving. But she couldn't be alive and inside Payton, could she?

Payton shook her head hard, as if doing so might reset her scrambled brain. Maybe she was having some kind of emotional breakdown. Maybe everything that had seemed so real was just in her imagination. Maybe the guilt of betraying Marley had destroyed her emotional health.

The thought that none of this was real felt strangely comforting. She decided she would go to bed, get some sleep, and in the morning she would tell her mom that she was having a hard time dealing with Marley being missing and that maybe she should see a doctor. Payton took several deep breaths and stood up.

The awful meaty taste was still in her mouth. She needed to brush her teeth.

She squeezed the paste onto her toothbrush and regarded herself in the mirror. She still looked pale and exhausted, but she wasn't sweaty and feverish-looking like she had been before. She brushed her teeth and tongue, scrubbing away the taste of blood and animal fat. She rinsed with water, then swished some minty mouthwash for good measure.

That was better. She was going to get better. She just needed to ask for some help.

She splashed her face with warm water and started to dry it off. As she rubbed the towel against her throat, she felt something jump inside her neck.

She looked in the mirror. Lumps were rising beneath the skin of her throat, moving around and rearranging themselves. Her skin stretched, and her veins bulged.

No, Payton thought. *This isn't real. This isn't real*

because what I thought happened before wasn't real, either.

But the image in the mirror told a different story.

Payton put both hands on her throat to make sure what she was seeing wasn't an illusion. Some of the lumps were the size of grapes. Others were nearly the size of golf balls. They moved under her fingers when she pressed on them, darting like they were trying to avoid her touch.

She felt some kind of solid matter making its way up her throat, making it hard to breathe and impossible to yell for her parents, for someone to do something. She felt so alone.

Except she wasn't alone because of the intruding presence inside her.

She looked back at the mirror. Now there were lumps on her face, too, large ones, moving around, distorting her features, straining the taut skin until it threatened to split.

Her eyes bulged. Something was pushing hard behind them. She had never felt such intense pressure. Her eyes protruded out from her eyelids, opening so wide that she could see the orbs in their entirety, the whites, the dilated pupils, the bursting blood vessels.

Pulpy red slop seeped, then spewed from her eye sockets so forcefully that her eyeballs were propelled from her face like cannonballs blasting from a cannon. One hit the mirror with a wet slap while the other one landed with a splat in the basin of the sink.

Pressed together into a soft, solid mass, the bits of flesh and tissue squeezed from Payton's empty eye sockets like fresh sausage being extruded from a meat grinder. The slop fell to the floor in long tubes. She could see nothing, but she could feel the pressure in her head building even more as it became fuller and fuller until she feared it might explode.

The meaty remains of Payton's best friend poured from her mouth and sprayed out of her nostrils in a sneeze that splattered the red compressed innards onto the white bathroom tiles. Still, the pressure in her head grew, throbbing like a huge hammer was pounding her skull from the inside.

It was a strange sort of relief when the fleshy paste started squeezing out of her ears, too. The pressure reduced, leaving Payton so light-headed she couldn't stand. She had never fainted, but she feared she might. Unseeing, unhearing, unable to make any sound except a soft whimper in the back of her clogged throat, she collapsed to her knees on the bathroom floor. She fell into a mound of body-temperature meat mush. Her fingers groped through slivers of skin, gobbets of organs, fragments of bone, all that was left of the friend she had turned her back on. Payton couldn't scream, couldn't cry, but in between bouts of spewing out more crushed human remains, she did manage to whisper one name. *Marley.*

Payton sat up in bed with a start, stifling a scream. Her stomach roiled, and her diaphragm spasmed. Her mouth filled with bitter saliva. There was no way to hold it back anymore. She was finally going to lose her lunch. Violently.

She jumped out of bed and ran. She stopped at the bathroom door for a second, but then kept running. For some reason, she didn't want what was going to come out of her to be inside the house, not even if she flushed it down the toilet. The remains of the pizza that churned inside her felt polluting, contaminating. She wanted it gone. She ran downstairs and out the front door.

Once she was out on the porch, she took deep breaths of fresh air in hopes that it would ease her nausea. No such luck. She ran to the edge of the porch and retched into the bushes.

Patyon had never vomited so violently or for so long. Clutching the stair railing to hold herself up, she spewed and spewed until she feared she would soon be vomiting up her own internal organs.

Surely, she thought, *there could be nothing left inside her.* But then another wave would hit her, and there would be more.

Finally, there came several minutes of dry heaving. At last, she was empty.

She tiptoed back into the house and locked the front door behind her. Her goal was to get back in bed without her parents noticing she had gone out. She was not in the mood to answer anybody's questions. All she wanted was to be left alone and to leave the terrible experiences of this day behind her.

Lying back down, she felt marginally better. She was weak and sweaty and shaky, but at least her stomach wasn't tossing like a ship in a stormy sea. And emotionally, there was something cleansing about the nightmare pizza having been purged from her system. It felt like a fresh start somehow. Payton closed her eyes, hoping she could sleep the night through.

But there was a noise.

It was a rustling noise coming from outside in the vicinity of the bushes where Payton had emptied herself of the vile pizza. *It's probably just squirrels or one of the neighborhood cats*, Payton thought. It would stop soon.

The rustling didn't stop. Instead, it got louder, making it impossible for Payton to sleep.

She got out of bed, went to her window, and opened it. The sound was definitely coming from the bushes where she'd been sick.

But wait. What if it was Marley?

After this thought, the horrible *what ifs* began to unspool in her brain. What if Marley wasn't coming back to joyously greet her friend? What if Marley was mad at her for not trying to save her? For not telling anyone, even the police officer, that she had seen Marley fall? Payton knew from experience that Marley had a temper and held grudges against people when she thought they had wronged her. What if Marley was out for revenge?

Another even more horrific thought spread like a stain in Payton's head. What if Marley had fallen into the vat of boiling sauce and died, but had somehow managed to come back, like in the dream she had just had? If it even had been a dream. What if what was outside was not really Marley but somehow *what was left* of Marley?

The doorbell rang.

Payton's heart pounded in panic. She had to get away, but how? Unable to think of another choice, she opened the window and climbed out onto the ivy-covered lattice on the side of the house. One piece of wood shattered under her bare foot. The lattice clearly wasn't strong enough to support her for long. Still, she clung to it with a white-knuckled grip.

She had climbed out of the window with the thought of shimmying down the side of the house and running away. But now she realized that going down the lattice would put her right next to the front porch. Right next to Marley.

There was no place to go but up.

The lattice shook and squeaked as she climbed

toward the roof. She grabbed the gutter and pulled herself up. She was so terrified she could hardly breathe. But even though she was afraid of heights, she was even more afraid of what was standing on her porch.

It'll be okay, she told herself. *I'll just sit on the roof till she's gone, then I'll climb back through the window into my room.*

She flinched as she heard the doorbell ring again.

Marley stood on the porch, waiting for the door to open.

Being missing had been kind of fun. No school, no responsibilities. But hiding out in the pizza factory had started to get old. She missed her boyfriend, missed regular meals, and missed sleeping in her own bed. She had gone to see her boyfriend first, and now she was going to let Payton know she was okay. Those visits were the first two phases of becoming un-missing. Then she would go back home for the required tearful reunion with her parents.

Thunk!

The sound came from the other side of the house. Marley ran down the porch steps to investigate.

It was dark around the back of the house, so it took Marley a moment to make sense of the shape lying on the ground. But then she saw it was a girl about her size. Her neck was twisted, and her head was tilted at a painful-looking angle. Payton's eyes, wide open in a frozen look of terror, seemed to be looking right at Marley. But Marley knew Payton wasn't looking at her, would never look at anything again.

Marley screamed.

ABOUT THE AUTHORS

Scott Cawthon is the author of the bestselling video game series *Five Nights at Freddy's*, and while he is a game designer by trade, he is first and foremost a storyteller at heart. He is a graduate of The Art Institute of Houston and lives in Texas with his family.

Elley Cooper writes fiction for young adults and adults. She has always loved horror and is grateful to Scott Cawthon for letting her spend time in his dark and twisted universe. Elley lives in Tennessee with her family and many spoiled pets and can often be found writing books with Kevin Anderson & Associates.

Larson was bent over his desk writing up a report on a manslaughter he and Roberts had cleared that morning. Roberts wasn't helping at all. He was berating Powell for bringing a Limburger cheese and liverwurst sandwich for lunch. Larson had to admit the smell was pretty bad, but Roberts wasn't being paid to be the scent police.

Larson was nearly done, even without Roberts's help. He was filling in the last section when a folder landed on his desk with an audible *slap*.

"Heard ya'll were waiting for these here results?"

The heavy drawl lifted Larson's gaze.

One of the new detectives, Chancey—Larson wasn't sure if this was a first or a last name—stood next to Larson's desk. He was tapping one of his cowboy-boot–clad feet on the scuffed floor.

Chancey was an angular guy with a jutting jaw and bony shoulders, dirty-blond hair that hung over his eyes, and a grin that looked even less genuine than his drawl sounded. Chancey had joined the squad while Larson was in the hospital. Larson had heard the guy was just supposed to be a fill-in for Larson while he was gone, but for some reason, Chancey was still here.

"This something I could get in on?" Chancey asked. "Looks hinky to me. Is it a cold case?"

Larson flipped open the folder and scanned the top page inside. He shook his head. "It's just something I was following up on. I'll let you know if I need your help." He gave Chancey a fake-friendly smile and pushed the folder aside as if it was nothing.

Chancey shrugged and wandered away from the bull pen. Larson opened the folder and studied its contents.

He started frowning as soon as he began reading. What in the world was going on here?

Larson had sent thirty samples to the lab. He'd expected to be told they were blood samples, and he'd expected them to be thirty different blood samples.

He was only half right. The samples were blood, but they weren't different. Well, they were different, but they weren't from different individuals.

The blood samples, according to the report, were from the same person, but they were all from different time periods. This meant someone—the same someone—or the same something, had bled in that pit every year for decades. *Huh?*

Larson picked up the phone and punched in a number. After a ring, a woman answered in a sing-songy voice.

"Lab, Tabitha here."

"Hey, Tabby. I'm looking at the report you sent over." He tapped the pages in front of him. "Are you telling me that something has been coming in and out of that ball pit for over three decades, and it's been bleeding?"

"It's weird, for sure," Tabby said. "But yeah, the blood is from the same person, but each sample has degraded differently, indicating a different year for each one. You're onto something funky, Larson."

"That's one word for it. Thanks, Tabby."

Larson hung up the phone and leaned back.

Something bigger was going on here, bigger even than having baffling glimpses into the past. He needed to find out more about the building where he'd found the pit. Maybe solving this mystery would lead him back to the Stitchwraith. Strangeness seemed to radiate outward from the freakish thing. Whether the Stitchwraith was evil or not, Larson wanted to find it and get to the bottom of whatever the heck was going on.

Jake pushed through the shed's doorway. He carried a lumpy bundle wrapped up in the folds of his cloak.

Although the previous night's rain had stopped, the sky was still heavy with gray clouds. The sun was trying to break through them, but so far, it wasn't having any success. Very little light made its way through the doorway into the small space when Jake stepped inside.

Even in the murk, though, Jake could see that the girl was no longer curled up on the floor. She was sitting up.

Jake closed the door and slowly approached the girl. He tried to hunch a little so his size wouldn't intimidate her.

But he shouldn't have bothered. The girl looked up at him with no fear at all.

"Hi," the girl said in a sweet, scratchy voice.

She'd said "hi" as if she was talking to a normal kid. So Jake responded as if he was.

"Hi. I'm Jake. What's your name?"

"Jake," the girl said. "That's a nice name. I'm Renelle."

"That's a nice name, too," Jake said. "Very pretty."

As he spoke, though, Jake felt funny about the

girl's name. It sounded wrong to him, like it didn't fit her or something. But that was silly.

"Thanks," the girl said.

Jake watched her and mentally repeated her name. Something sounded off about it, like it was a half-truth.

The girl smiled at Jake.

Jake stopped worrying about her name. He squatted down next to her and dumped the canned goods he'd foraged onto the floor next to her. She immediately reached out, grabbed a tin of tuna, and tugged on its pull tab.

"I'm starving," Renelle said as she scooped tuna from the can with her fingers.

Jake couldn't stop smiling. She looked so much better! Color was back in her cheeks. Her eyes were bright and animated.

Renelle had obviously finger-combed her hair and straightened her clothing while Jake was gone. Her face was cleaner, so she must have spit-scrubbed it.

Weirdly, it looked like Renelle wasn't as skinny as she'd been when Jake had left her, but that was obviously impossible. Jake figured that Renelle's renewed energy made her look more substantial than she had when she was passed out.

While Renelle ate, she looked around. "Where are we?" she asked with her mouth full. When she realized what she'd done, she giggled and covered her mouth with her hand. "Sorry."

Jake laughed. "It's okay." He looked around the shed. "We're near the railroad tracks. I wanted to get you someplace no one comes to, away from those men."

Renelle's pretty blue eyes widened. "What men?"

"The two men who looked like they wanted to hurt you." He hesitated. Should he tell her what he thought? He decided he should. He wanted them to be friends, and he was always honest with his friends. "I think they were your dealers?"

Renelle had finished the tuna, and she was reaching for a can of peaches. She stopped and sucked in her breath. Her gaze darted toward the door. "Where are they now?"

"Don't worry. I took care of them. They're not going to find you here."

Renelle returned her gaze to Jake. She shivered once but then nodded. "Thanks." She popped open the peaches and began slurping peach juice.

Jake was amazed that Renelle didn't seem at all bothered by his appearance. She was treating him like an ordinary boy. "You're not afraid of me!" Jake blurted.

"You helped me, and besides . . ." Renelle ate a peach slice and looked Jake up and down. After she swallowed, she said, "I've been on the street long enough to know that what we think of as monsters—things that might look like you—aren't the real monsters. Most real monsters are people, especially guys who think they can push around girls like me just because I don't have a place to live. But you? You're not a monster. You just look different."

"I'm glad you think that," Jake said.

He watched her eat. He wanted to ask her questions, but he wasn't sure if it was polite.

Renelle finished the peaches and licked her fingers. She looked at Jake. "You're wondering why I'm a druggie."

Jake shook his head, but she was right. He did wonder.

Renelle crossed her legs and hugged herself. "My mom died when I was thirteen."

Jake sat down next to Renelle. He thought about touching her hand, but he wasn't sure he should. "I'm sorry," he said. "I know what that's like. My mom died, too. It's awful."

Renelle touched Jake's cloak. "I'm sorry, too. Yes, it is." Her gaze drifted off past Jake's shoulder. "That was just two years ago, but it feels like forever. I was really close to my mom, and when she died, I was a mess and no one was there for me."

"What about your dad?" Jake asked.

Renelle shook her head. "He was all wrapped up in his own grief, and he couldn't deal, you know? He disappeared into his work, got obsessive about it. He couldn't help me." She sighed. "I tried to cope. I really did. But I finally couldn't stand the pain anymore."

Renelle smiled at him. "You're really nice. My dad didn't understand at all. He hauled me off to one of those schools for kids who get in trouble, and he left me there. When I got out, he was still wrapped up in his work. I stole some of his money, and when he found out I'd done that, he kicked me out. Told me not to come back."

"I'm so sorry."

Renelle shrugged and reached for another can, this one a small tin of deviled ham. She opened it and scooped out some of the salty-smelling pink meat. She chewed, swallowed, and wiped her mouth with the back of her hand.

Renelle concentrated on eating, but her eyes were shiny with tears. Jake could tell she loved her dad and missed him. He could intensely feel her loss.

Watching Renelle polish off the deviled ham, Jake decided he was going to find Renelle's father and get them reunited. He didn't know how, but he was going to figure it out.

The moment Jake made his decision, the sun won its battle with the clouds. A ray of golden light shot in through the shed's smudged window and landed on Renelle.

The light made Renelle look like a sweet angel. And it revealed something Jake hadn't noticed before.

Renelle was wearing a very unusual pendant. Hanging from a silver chain, the pendant was a somewhat misshapen silver heart. The puffy shape reminded Jake of things he'd seen in comic strips; this heart was the kind of heart he'd expect a cartoon character to wear.

The way the sun hit the silver made it glint and flash sparkles. The sparkles made Jake smile. He thought it was a sign that something good was going to happen.